SAM

LINDA FORD

1

Circle A Ranch, 1887

"You want me to do what?" Sam had heard his sister correctly but didn't believe the words. She wanted him to take Yvette Bellamy to town?

"I know the two of you haven't hit it off but you're my brother and she's my best friend. I'd really like it if you'd try to be friends with her."

Haven't hit it off? That was an understatement. Little Miss Rich Girl was barely civil to him. Of course, she wasn't rude. Her upbringing forbade that. But her haughty looks conveyed clearing her feelings.

"Do it for me."

Grace knew she could ask him most anything and he'd do it. But this? "I doubt she'd agree to go with me."

"I asked her and she already has."

He wasn't fooled by the innocent look on his sister's face. "What did you say?"

"Sam, I know you'd like her if you gave her half a chance. She's a sweet, loyal person who's been badly hurt."

"Huh?" It wasn't like *he'd* done anything to hurt her.

"People take advantage of her because her father is rich. I told you of her ex-beau who only courted her to gain favor with Mr. Bellamy."

"Uh-huh. And me taking a trip to town with her is supposed to correct that?"

"Sam, give her a chance. Besides, you're going anyway. I heard John tell you to take one of the teams to town and get them shod. She can go with you."

She had him trapped.

"Very well. Just don't expect we'll suddenly become all friendly."

"Guess I can hope. And pray."

He laughed. "No doubt she'll be praying the opposite."

Grace flicked her hand at him. "Oh, you." She paused. Her smile disappeared. "Sam?"

Her change of tone made his thumbs curl.

"She's been making some odd statements lately. I put it down as a reaction to how she is so often treated, but please make sure she goes to where the Parkers are waiting for her."

He understood the Parkers were a couple who were to escort Yvette back to her parents. They'd rented a little house in Logan Crossing to wait for her.

"What kind of odd statements?" Before she could answer, he wondered what she thought he would do with Miss Yvette. "Where else would I take her?"

Grace shrugged. "Just promise you'll take her to the Parkers."

"Fine. I'll make sure she gets to them." It was an easy promise to make. There was no place between the ranch and Logan Crossing where they could go.

An hour later he had the team hitched to the wagon, Miss Yvette's bags in the back and he assisted the fine lady to the wagon seat. He climbed up beside her and waved goodbye to Grace.

They crossed the bridge and climbed the hill, the ranch at their back. He settled down into himself. Sixty minutes, more or less, to town. He could live with his own thoughts until then.

"I'm glad to have this chance to talk to you."

Yvette's words jerked him from his musing. Before he could say he didn't think they had anything to talk about, she continued.

"I find it very difficult, if not impossible, to understand why you had Adam write to Grace and let her think it was you."

She'd no doubt heard the whole story. It had started innocently enough. Years ago, Grace had been adopted into a family. Sam knew how difficult his sister found it to adjust and wanted to write and encourage her. When Adam saw how Sam struggled to pen a letter, he'd offered to help. But it had continued far too long. Sam regretted not being honest. "Seems to me it turned out all right." Grace had met Adam. They'd fallen in love and were now happily married.

The flick of Yvette's eyebrows said plainly she didn't agree. Nor was she about to leave it. "I hardly think you can take credit for that. Does it not say in First Corinthians that God hath chosen the foolish things of the world to confound the wise?"

He stared straight ahead, his eyes on the horses, his mind on trying to muddle out what she meant. It sounded to him like she was calling him a fool but allowing that God used his actions to the surprise of everyone. His rib cage sank to his belt. Guess he couldn't argue with that.

"Grace understands. We've made peace with it."

"I simply don't know why people can't be honest."

Her words fell like tiny pebbles on the surface of a still lake. Little ripples spread out in widening circles. He kind of figured each ripple represented something more than what the word said. "Grace told me about your ex-beau. I'm sorry. But that was different."

She turned to face him, her hazel eyes wide. Her brown hair was neatly coiled at the back of her head. Every hair perfectly in place. She was nineteen, a year younger than himself, yet she made him feel like an uncouth youth. Not that she said or did anything.

Guess he couldn't blame her for his own insecurities that surfaced around her.

He pushed aside his thoughts and focused on her eyes. His breath caught as he glimpsed pain in her gaze. And then a coldness glazed it.

"How is it different? Truth is truth. Honesty is honesty. Anything else is despicable."

For a moment, he was speechless. Words didn't come easy for him. Seemed he could never bridge the gulf between his thoughts and his tongue. "Well, you'll soon be back at your home."

"Where truth and honesty are rare." She shifted around to stare straight ahead. "I think I can only find truth by finding someone who doesn't know me."

He squinted at her. Was Grace right? Did she have something planned?

She jerked back to study him. "I thought cowboys were honest to the bone. You've disabused me of that idea."

"Hey, wait a minute. I never meant to be dishonest. I only wanted to cheer my sister up. Then it seemed needlessly cruel to tell her it wasn't me. I didn't expect her to travel out here and discover the truth herself."

She opened her mouth to say something but he rushed on.

"That doesn't make cowboys dishonest. Any more than being a cowboy makes a man honest."

"You have a point." Her shoulder sagged. "It's so hard to know…to judge."

Why did her disappointment and uncertainty mean anything to him? After he delivered her to the Parkers he'd never see her again. The thought should have given him relief.

But it didn't.

He wished he could help her. Show her that cowboys were good people. Make her forget how that ex-beau had used her.

Instead, he pointed out the landmarks. And she seemed to be interested though she might only be pretending in order to be polite. If he knew her better, he might point out that, too, lacked honesty.

The town came into sight.

He drove to the little house at the edge of town, set back from the dusty street behind a row of overgrown caragana bushes. He helped her down and lifted her bags from the wagon.

"I'll take them inside," he said.

"No need. Put them on the step. Thank you for the ride." She waited.

He didn't move. "Grace specially asked me to deliver you to the Parkers."

She huffed with royal indignation. "You're either saying you don't trust me or you don't think I can make it through the door without your help. Humph. Maybe you're saying both. I'll have you know I am not a pampered helpless woman." She drew herself up tall and righteous. "I don't appreciate your judgment."

"Fine. Have it your way." He was not going to stand on the step arguing with her. Nor was he going to force her aside so he could open the door and take her things in.

Instead, he set the bags on the step and returned to the wagon, drove it to the blacksmith shop where he unhitched the team and made arrangements for the horses to be shod. Then he strode to the store thinking how good a peppermint stick would taste about now. Neutralize some of the bitter taste in his mouth from dealing with Miss Yvette. She thought he was judging her? It was quite the opposite. She judged him and not in a kindly way.

Ilsa greeted him as he entered the store. "What brings you to town?"

He explained about the horses. "And I brought Miss Yvette. She and the Parkers are to travel back to Winnipeg."

Ilsa had been about to take a peppermint stick out of the jar for him but she withdrew her empty hand and stared at Sam.

"The Parkers left two days ago."

Sam sure could use that candy right now to suck moisture into his mouth. But surely he'd misheard. "What do you mean they're gone? I just dropped her off there." He thumped his forehead. "I should have walked her inside." He'd offered to. Yvette had said it wasn't necessary. And Yvette was used to having her wishes obeyed.

Grace was right to think Yvette had something planned.

"I better find out what's going on." He had no desire to explain to Grace that he'd failed after she'd been very specific about her instructions.

Calling thanks over his shoulder, he raced from the store and back to the little house. Behind bushes, back from the street, it was the perfect place to arrange a secret meeting. It baffled him as to how and when Yvette would have arranged such a thing. But something wasn't right. That was for sure. She'd tricked him into thinking she was going home as expected. Obviously, she had other plans.

He didn't care to admit how easily he'd been duped.

His knuckles met rough weathered wood as he banged on the door and, without waiting for an answer, he barged in. If she was up to mischief he meant to catch her in the act. Though he had no idea what he thought she might be doing.

"Miss Bellamy, you said—" His protest choked off as he stared into the barrel of a handgun.

"Shoulda minded yer own business," the body behind the gun growled.

Sam's hands reached for the ceiling. His lungs gasped for air. He blinked hard and squinted at the man. Thick-bodied, mean-faced. A cruel twist to his mouth. Scraggly black hair jutting out from under a greasy flat cap that might have once been brown.

Sam had met a few men like him. Weaselly and nasty.

"What do you want?" He kept his voice firm and steady. Showing any weakness before men like the one he stared at only made them bigger bullies. He'd learned that lesson well at the orphanage.

"Don't want company but here ya is."

Sam glanced past the man. The room was empty save for Yvette's bags that had been dropped by the door. Two doorways led off this room. He saw nothing in either of them.

A thumping like something being kicked came from the far room. And a muffled sound like someone calling from deep inside a closet. Was Yvette in there? Why didn't she come out? One possibility occurred to him. This was a man bent on evil. Had he hurt her? The roots of his hair tingled at the thought. He'd had one job. See she got home safely. And he'd failed. His brain scrambled for options.

"Guess I'll be on my way." He began to lower his arms and turn but the gun pressed closer.

"Ya ain't goin' nowheres."

Sam stopped. Not that he'd thought he'd be allowed to leave but it was worth a try.

He stared at the man. The man stared back with his tiny, narrow eyes. What next?

"Ya've put a knot in my plans. Guess now I'll have to take ya too."

"Where're we going?" Sam hoped he sounded curious, interested even, as his mind spun, examining every route of escape and finding none that seemed at all appealing. He had no wish to die. Besides, if the man shot him, he wouldn't be any help to Yvette. If she needed help. Perhaps this was all arranged ahead of time. Nah. He couldn't believe Yvette would have any association with a man like the one facing him.

"Never ya mind." The man jabbed his gun to his right. "Jest head that there direction."

Sam eased past the weasel, watching for any sign of inattention on the man's part but no opportunity to grab the gun appeared. He entered a smaller room. A bare mattress on steel springs indicated it was a bedroom. The absence of bedding or belongings informed him the occupants had left.

Yvette sat on the floor, tied and gagged. She thumped her heels and sent daggers from her eyes that should have cut the man into a thousand pieces but failed to do anything except bring a chortle.

She shifted her piercing gaze toward Sam.

He shook his head. There was no sense in blaming him. He had nothing to do with this.

Their captor ordered Sam to lower his arms. He grabbed a rope and looped it around Sam's wrists.

Knowing the man would need both hands to tie him up, Sam sprang away. Now when the man was distracted was his chance to get the gun. But before he got close enough, the gun was aimed at his head.

"Nuff funny bizness. Ya wanna go. Ya go." He

shifted direction and pressed the gun barrel to Yvette's temple. "The first step ya take, I blow her head off. How'd ya like that?"

Sam held his hands up in a gesture of submission. "No need to get fussed. What is it you want?"

"I heared about this gal. She's worth a pile of money."

Yvette sat very still. All except her eyes which burned rage at both men.

"Really?" Sam aimed for indifference even though anger and alarm surged through his veins. "Could be you heard wrong."

"Nah. Heared the people livin' here talkin'. Figger I can get a bundle for her."

"Only if she's alive."

Sam could tell by the way the man's eyes shifted from him to Yvette that he hadn't considered that.

Then he shook his head. "Not ta worry. Blackie here knows what he's doin'. Got him a good plan."

"You're Blackie?" Or did he work for another?

The man's chest puffed out. "That'd be me. Sure ya've heared of me."

Sam decided it wise not to say he'd never heard of him and could have happily lived the rest of his life without ever doing so. He gave a non-committal tilt of his head. "Maybe I have. Maybe I haven't."

Blackie let the gun ease back from Yvette's temple. "Could get my name in every paper in the country by killing ya both."

"Likely get yourself hung too." Hardness spread throughout Sam. Blackie wasn't going to kill either of them if Sam had anything to say about it. There had to be a way to outsmart the man and he meant to find it.

"They'd have ta catch me first."

"Hard to enjoy your moment of fame if you're hiding. Say, I have an idea. Why don't you and I become partners? Two of us working together are more likely to succeed. We'll split the ransom money."

Yvette squirmed around until her feet aimed in Sam's direction. She grunted as she tried to kick him. The look in her eyes impaled him with threats of a thousand deaths.

He met her look, trying to signal that it was a ruse. He would never be partners with Blackie but if Blackie believed he was…well, wouldn't it give Sam a way to rescue Yvette?

Yvette couldn't talk but that didn't prevent her from choking out sounds that rang with fury.

Blackie shuffled from foot to foot considering Sam's offer. Then his eyes narrowed. "I don't share my money with nobody. Now less get on with bizness."

He jerked Yvette to her feet and held her with one hand, the gun still in his other. "You go first." He nodded toward Sam. "What's yer name?"

"Sam." If he ended up dead, he wanted the proper name scratched on a piece of wood.

"Fine. Sam, go out the back door. We'll be right

behind ya. Ya try any funny bizness and I'll shoot her first and then you next. Got it?"

"I got it." Guess so long as Blackie figured Sam didn't want him shooting Yvette, he would give him some freedom. He meant to use that to his advantage.

Blackie kicked Yvette's luggage out the door and followed Sam.

There were two horses tied at the little shelter.

"Only figgered to need two hosses." Blackie sounded unhappy about the arrangement. "But it'll be all right." He looped the rope holding Yvette over a fence post effectively making it impossible for her to attempt an escape. Then he turned the gun toward Sam. "Sam, you get on that hoss."

Sam swung into the saddle. Blackie had neglected to tie his hands as he meant to do a short time ago. It would take but one kick in the horse's ribs for Sam to bolt. But the gun was leveled at his head and Sam wasn't about to test Blackie to see how good a shot he was.

A time would come when he could escape. He'd either go for help alone or take Yvette with him. That would no doubt prove interesting in ways he didn't care to experience.

Blackie looped the rope around Sam's ankle, drew the rope under the horse, and looped it around the other foot. Well, at least, Sam thought, he couldn't fall off. Blackie tied Sam's wrists so tight Sam knew it would cut off the circulation. But his hands were in front so he would be able to ride somewhat comfortably. But he'd rejoiced too soon. Blackie bound Sam's wrists together then clipped a rope to the horse's bridle. So Sam was to be led.

Blackie brought the other horse to the fence. He hung her satchels on the saddle and then hoisted Yvette in front of the saddle, her legs to one side.

Sam knew it would be an uncomfortable position. On top of that, he was certain she had never been handle so roughly in her life.

He felt a smidgen of sympathy for her. But she might need to endure even worse treatment if they didn't escape. And, perhaps, even if they did.

YVETTE'S THROAT was so parched it hurt and tickled so badly she wanted to cough but she held back the urge. She could barely swallow with that dirty rag stuffed in her mouth. Ropes cut into her ankles. Warmth in the area caused her to suspect they'd cut through her skin. With her arms tied behind her, it was all she could do to stay balanced on the back of that horse.

Fury raged through her, warring with fear. She'd hoped she'd suffered enough for having a rich father. Arbitrary rules that made no sense and were difficult to follow, often robbing her of any enjoyment in an event. But learning that Morgan only courted her to gain financial favor with her father made her realize just how little she was valued for herself. Apart from friends like Grace.

Poor Grace. Sam had deceived her once by pretending to write letters he hadn't but for him to want to take part in kidnapping her! Was that why he'd wanted to escort her inside? She reviewed the events. If he'd been involved in the kidnapping, wouldn't he have ignored her protests? And now he was tied up. So obviously he wasn't involved. But even so, that didn't change anything. He'd *offered* to be part of her kidnapping. No doubt for financial gain or simply to save his own neck. Sam was despicable. Willing to use anyone and anything for his benefit.

If she ever got out of this, she would see that Sam paid dearly for his behavior.

Not if. When.

How could he be Grace's brother? Grace would be so hurt. Yvette couldn't imagine having a brother she couldn't trust. *There is a friend that sticketh closer than a brother.* How badly she needed the assurance that God saw her predicament and would never leave her nor forsake her. *Lord God, send help. Rescue me from mine enemy.*

Blackie swung up behind her in the saddle. He reached over to take the rope tied to Sam's horse and tied it to Yvette's wrists. He cackled with wicked glee.

"Your friend try and get away he'll drag you from the horse."

He's not my friend, she silently screamed. Her

shoulders burned from having her hands tied behind her. If Sam so much as fell back one foot, her arms would snap from their sockets.

Not that she supposed he'd care.

Blackie's arms reached around her as he took the reins. Not surprisingly, he had a rank odor. "Ain't this cozy?" His breath was foul.

She closed her eyes and choked back the rising nausea. The man was disgusting. Tears welled up but she held them back. Bible verses she'd memorized filled her thoughts. *In my distress, I cried unto the Lord and he heard me. Deliver my soul, O Lord.* She clung to the hope and promise of those words as they bounced along the trail away from town.

If she needed any more proof of Sam's complicity, the fact he didn't even call out to anyone in the nearby houses provided it.

Oh Lord, be my shelter and protector.

The words were a desperate cry. There was no one else to help her.

As soon as they were out of sight of town, Blackie nudged his horse to a faster pace. "Best ya keep up less'n ya want to see her arms ripped off." He lowered his voice. "Could be he don't care seein' as I refused to cut him in."

Not exactly reassuring words but neither were they a new thought.

"I'll do my best to keep up," Sam called, whether for her benefit or Blackie's, she couldn't say.

"Figgered ya would. Less'n yer sore about me not cutting ya in."

Sam didn't answer and Yvette guessed Blackie had hit on the truth.

They rode onward. After a few minutes, Sam called again. "Where are we going?"

"Ain't none of yer bizness. Now no more talkin'." He jerked on the lead rope and Yvette moaned at the pain in her shoulders.

Thankfully, Sam kept his mouth shut after that.

They crossed the creek and turned to the right. They were soon making their way along a ridge of ground bordered with trees following a narrow trail of some sort. Then they were climbing among rocks. Fatigue and pain joined her fear and anger as she struggled to stay upright without leaning on Blackie's arms.

"Mmmmfff," was the only sound she could get out. Why wouldn't he remove the gag? They were miles from anyone who would hear her cry for help.

The trail grew more rugged, forcing Blackie to concentrate. Thankfully, he'd taken to holding the rope from Sam's horse in one hand so there wasn't a constant jerking on her arms.

They rode onward as the sun circled the sky, passing the zenith and heading toward the west.

Blackie obviously did not feel the need for a break for any reason. They'd ridden past dinnertime, and it looked like they'd continue riding past suppertime.

The world dipped to one side. Only it wasn't the world dipping, it was Yvette falling asleep. Thudding in her head suggested she was feeling faint. She blinked hard and forced slow breaths into her lungs and the dizziness disappeared.

"Horses are getting weary," Sam called.

It was the first words he'd spoken since Blackie's warning.

"They can wait until I's ready to stop."

"It will soon be dark," Sam pointed out as if the others hadn't noticed the black shadows reaching across the trail. If one could call it a trail. In places Blackie had to duck to keep the low-hanging branches from swatting him.

Dusk deepened further, but they continued on. Yvette lost all sense of direction and distance. All she knew was they were in rocky, treed terrain.

Yvette's head dipped forward, increasing the tension on her shoulders and jerking her back to alertness.

"We's here."

Yvette blinked. Saw nothing but dark shadows.

Where were they?

2

Sam watched helplessly as Blackie dropped Yvette to the ground. She swayed, but, to her credit, did not fall. Blackie turned to Sam and untied him. He stood on the ground, his feet full of pins and needles. His hands were still bound or he would have reached out to Yvette to steady her.

Their captor jerked her gag out of her mouth.

Yvette tried to speak, but all that came out was a croak.

Sam's insides burned at the way Blackie chortled. As if he took delight in her pain. A true bully.

Blackie untied her wrists.

Yvette moaned as she pulled her arms forward.

The idea of causing her the pain Sam knew she'd be experiencing made him hold back a growl. He had not felt so helpless in a very long time.

Blackie untied her ankles and straightened then he

moved away, his movements merely shadows in the low light. Sam heard something heavy move then Blackie said, "Boys, where's the light?"

Boys? There were more of them? Sam didn't like those odds.

The flickering light of a candle revealed a low doorway.

"Come on in and make yerselves at home." Blackie cackled again. He grabbed Sam's bound wrists and one of Yvette's arms and shoved them through the opening.

Sam stumbled. Yvette groaned and clutched his arm to keep from falling. He didn't need to be told her feet were as numb as his, if not worse.

The candle flame shone upon the face of a child. And peeking past the first child, was the face of a second.

They were truly boys. Just boys. He couldn't see them well enough to guess their age, but their size suggested they were not as big as Boyd at the ranch, who was twelve.

Blackie lit another candle, illuminating the room enough for Sam to see they were in a solid log structure with only four narrow slits that were black at the present but in the day would let in light. This cabin appeared to be a fortress of sorts. As if to prove his assumption, Blackie closed the door and did something at the bottom. It looked to Sam like he'd somehow locked the door.

Sam shivered despite the warmth of the room.

"You boys been behavin' yerselves?" Blackie demanded.

"Yes, Uncle," they chorused.

Blackie freed Sam's wrists then turned to the children. "Whatcha got to eat?"

The bigger of the boys rushed to a small cupboard. "Got some beans," he said, his voice thin. "I'll heat us up some." He hustled toward a tiny wood heater, threw a piece of log on the coals and soon had a little fire going. He opened a large can of beans and set it on top of the stove.

"Got water? Spect this lady is thirsty."

The younger boy jerked up and down on the handle of a pump near the cupboard.

Seeing the supply cupboard, the wood for the fire, and a source of water, Sam thought they could survive being trapped here if it came to that. And the way shudders crept up and down his spine, he wondered if it would.

The boy filled a pail with water and lifted a dipperful to Yvette. She drank greedily. "Thank you," she said when she had finished the second dipperful. "What's your name?"

"Tad."

Blackie growled and Tad hurried away. "Them's my nephews. Tad and Gil. Don't be trying to get all friendly with them. They works for me."

Sam's insides burned at Blackie's words. "What sort of work would that be?"

"Ya'd be amazed at what a man can do when people is busy feelin' sorry for two young uns." Blackie laughed as if it was the greatest joke.

Sam's fist clenched and his jaw muscles bunched.

Beside him, he felt Yvette's indrawn breath and saw her open her mouth. "Leave it be," he murmured. Blackie was distracted by rooting through the cupboards, so he dared to say more in a barely audible whisper. "We need to do our best to stay on his good side. It's our only hope he'll let his guard down."

Even in the flickering candlelight he saw her piercing, accusing look. He wished he could explain his actions to her and why he'd offered to be part of her kidnapping. But he could hardly say anything in front of Blackie.

"Anyone hungry?" the man asked. "Suppose ya be wantin' fancy dishes." He laughed loudly.

Gil quietly got two bowls, took them to the stove and put in beans. He handed the bowls to Yvette and Sam along with two battered spoons.

Blackie dug into the can of beans with his knife while the boys stood by, waiting.

Sam suddenly lost his appetite. "You boys can have my rations."

Blackie waved the knife at Sam. "You stays away from my kids. I tells 'em what to do. They knows they wait 'til I eat. Then they can have wha's left."

Sam ate beans that landed like lead in his stomach. He'd known lean meals in the orphanage and mean-spirited men. But if Blackie was indeed their uncle, shouldn't he be a little more charitable toward them? Instead, he took his time about eating, licking the knife with deliberate slowness, then satisfied, he sat back on the only chair in the place and waved the boys forward. The two cleaned out the can.

"Ain't much room, but we'll all find a place to sleep. Jest as soon as I make water." He went outside and slammed the door closed. The thud of a heavy bar let everyone inside know they wouldn't be dashing out to freedom.

Yvette let out a sigh that must have come from yesterday it was so drawn out. "Is there a bedroom?"

Gil shook his head. "Uncle sleeps on the cot when he's here. Me and Tad sleep on the floor." He pointed toward a pile of gray blankets.

Yvette wobbled and Sam caught her arm to steady her. She jerked away. "I can't believe you're part of this."

"I'm not. I only thought asking to be might give us a chance to escape."

She drew her brows together. "Seems to me you were only thinking of yourself. Always taking the easy way out no matter whether it's honest or not."

"That's not fair." Would she ever leave the matter of his pretend letter writing in the past? "I promised Grace I would see you safely to the Parkers and I intend to do my best to fulfill that promise." Before she could answer, he turned to the boys. "Is Blackie truly your uncle?" It crossed his mind that the boys might also be kidnapped.

"Mama's brother," Gil said. "Mama always said he'd chosen the wrong path."

"Where are your parents?" The boys could still be kidnapped.

"Dead. Late last winter. Uncle is our only relative." Gil pulled Tad to his side.

If they'd been with Blackie since then, it would be at least six months. The poor children. "How old are you?"

Gil again answered for the two of them. "I'm eleven. Tad is seven."

Sam studied the children. Both were thin to the point of gauntness. Tad had light brown hair. Likely lighter in color when clean. And blue eyes filled with hope and trust. Gil was darker, with brown hair and brown eyes that revealed resigned despair.

The door rattled, creaked, and groaned and Blackie stepped inside. He paused at the door and again fiddled with something on the floor. "See ya're all here still." He laughed as he crossed toward the cot.

"I need to go outside," Yvette said in a demanding voice.

"Is that a fact? Well, these boys manage for days without going out. See that bucket in the corner? Use it."

"I can not only see it. I smell it. And I won't use it."

"Suit yerself." He flung himself on the cot.

Yvette reached for the door.

A gunshot exploded. Sulfur filled the air. Two little boys cowered in the corner. Sam's ears rang.

Yvette sank to the ground, covering her head.

The bullet had lodged in the thick door, several inches above where Yvette's head would have been, but it was warning enough. Blackie was not a man to mess with, even though he lay on the bed looking as relaxed as if someone had read him a storybook.

Tad sidled up to Yvette and touched her shoulder.

Yvette jolted like his touch was a gunshot.

"You wanna use the bucket, we won't look. None of us."

Sam didn't know how he could speak for all of them, but he murmured he wouldn't look.

Yvette had never been so humiliated in her life. Nor so desperate. She had to relieve herself somewhere. That horrible man wasn't going to let her go outside. She stood and marched toward the odorous bucket. A slab of wood covered it. She removed it and almost gagged at the smell. How inhumane to force people to live like this. But she had no choice. She lifted her skirts and relieved herself. Her cheeks burned so hot it wouldn't have surprised her if they burst into flames.

She rearranged her skirts and did her best to hold her head high. After all, she was a Bellamy. Her shoulders sank. Being a Bellamy is why she was in this situation.

"Go to bed. All of ya," her horrible captor growled.

"And where, kind sir, shall we go to bed?"

Blackie sat up and swung his feet to the floor. "Lookee here. I ain't got nothin' fancy. Least not yet. Now when I gets paid for releasin' ya, I'll be able to buy nice things. Maybe ya'd like to pay me a visit then."

"Never."

"No mind. Gil, give them some of yer blankets."

Sam leaned close. "We'll have to sleep on the floor. Like the boys."

"Never." She said the word again with more heat.

"Suit yerself." Blackie lay down with absolutely no concern for anyone else.

Gil brought her a blanket. "It's not so bad once you get used to it."

She shuddered. But she hadn't forgotten her manners. "Thank you." But she stood holding the blanket and wondering when she would wake from this nightmare.

Tad came to her and took her hand. "You can have my bed." He guided her to the corner where she'd seen a tangle of blankets. Tad smoothed one out. "You lay there. You'll be all right. I'll watch over you."

The child's tenderness brought a sting of tears to her eyes and she thanked him. She drew her satchels to her. Inside were the only things of her normal life— her changes of clothing, her little Bible, and the newspaper clipping she'd tucked between the pages. Using one of her travel bags as a pillow, she lay down on the floor. It was far from comfortable, but then, most of this day had been far from comfortable.

A thin voice whispered close by. "'Savior, like a shepherd lead us, much we need Thy tender care. In Thy pleasant pastures feed us, for our use Thy folds prepare. Blessed Jesus, blessed Jesus, Thou hast bought us, Thine we are.'" The words were clear, sung in a voice fit for the heavens. Tad was surely an angel in disguise.

Jesus hadn't deserted her. He would take care of her.

YVETTE WAKENED to the rattle of the stove. Tad lay curled up beside her. She smiled. It was comforting to have her own little guardian angel. She sat up and glanced around.

Sam and Gil sat side by side between her and the bed where Blackie had slept.

No one moved but Blackie at the stove. Finished

with the fire, he cleaned his hands on his already soiled trousers and studied the four of them.

"Gil, get up and get rid of that smelly bucket. Take out the ashes too."

The boy was on his feet in a flash and out the door with the thing that had served as a toilet.

He left the door open to let in bright sunlight.

Yvette took careful study of the hovel they were in. It was smaller than a maid's room. Four slots for light. A cupboard which, no doubt, held supplies. Other than a chair, the cot, the tiniest stove she'd ever seen, and a stack of wood to be burned, that was it. Her bags beside her. At least she had those.

"How are you going to let my father know where I am?"

"Done that already. Sent the letter the same day the Fishers left. Blackie here done thought of ever'thin'."

"How are you getting the money?" She hoped her questions would make him realize there was a flaw in his plans. But if he did, why would he bother to keep her? Would he shoot her and leave her body to rot in the woods? She looked at Sam, hoping he had better thoughts than she did.

He kept a close eye on Blackie.

"I got it figgered out. Y'all see. You." He pointed at Yvette. "Make us some brea'fast."

She bolted to her feet. If she admitted she didn't know how to make anything except tea, what would he do?

Tad smiled at her. "It's easy," he said and went to the cupboard.

"Lady?" Blackie's low growl made Yvette hurry to join Tad.

Gil returned with the bucket. Then scurried out with the ashes.

Sam watched the proceedings then headed for the door.

The click of Blackie's gun stopped him in his tracks.

"Where ya think yer goin'?"

"Thought I'd help the boy with the wood."

"Boy's been doin' fine on his own."

"Just the same." Sam ducked through the door.

Yvette's hands clenched and she closed her eyes tight, waiting for the deafening sound of a gunshot.

Instead, Blackie snorted. "Ya better hope he comes back or y'all be the one to pay."

Sam would likely bolt the first chance he got, leaving her to deal with Blackie on her own. She ignored the irony of wanting him to stay and help her while blaming him for everything wrong in her life. Well, not everything, just the present circumstances. All right, she couldn't that wasn't entirely his fault, but it helped to have someone to blame.

Tad directed her attention to a sack of yellow granular flour. "Cornmeal is easy," he said. He pumped water into a pot, sprinkled in cornmeal, and set it on the stove to cook, stirring it all the while. "It's dead easy, is what Gil says."

Yvette didn't care for anything being *dead easy*. Dead was final and hovering far too close to her, but she figured she better watch what Tad did. Just to be on the safe side.

Gil and Sam returned with armloads of wood.

She favored Sam with a scalding look. Yet she was marginally grateful he had returned.

Gil washed the bowls from the night before and when the cornmeal mush was ready, served up bowlfuls for her and Sam.

"I'll pray." Sam bowed his head before the startled Blackie could protest. "God, you know everything. You see us and You've promised to take care of us. We thank you for that and for providing us with food for the day. Amen."

Without looking at Blackie, he began to eat.

Yvette took a mouthful of the breakfast and almost spit it out. She was used to sugar or raisins to sweeten something like this. But, suspecting she wouldn't be offered anything else, she swallowed.

Again, Blackie ate from the pot while the boys waited for him to get as much as he wanted.

He finished and rose to his feet. "I'll be gone this mornin'. Get us some meat. The boys will tell ya there's no way ya can get out of here." He grabbed up a saddlebag and stepped into the sunlight. He slammed the door, turning the inside into gloom and then something thudded on the outside.

"He puts up a heavy bar," Gil said. "I can't move it." He brightened as he looked at Sam. "You might be able to."

"Let's have a look."

The four of them went to the slab of wood that served as a door.

Sam looked. "This is how he keeps us in when he's here." There was a bar at the bottom of the door and a metal loop.

"He has a big padlock that he always has with him," Gil said.

Sam shoved on the door. He pulled on it. He leaned his shoulder to it and pushed. He tried to jiggle it. It didn't move. He sat back. "It's no use. I saw it when I was outside. A thick wooden bar. It's solid. And blocked at each end." He sighed. "But I had to try."

Despair drained all hope from Yvette's heart. "It's an impenetrable jail." She grabbed Sam's arm and pulled him as far away from the boys as was possible in this closet of a room.

"What if Blackie doesn't come back? This jail will become a tomb."

3

Sam looked around the room. The logs looked fairly fresh. And solid. If Blackie had built this cabin, he knew what he was doing. "I don't intend to die here," he murmured to Yvette. He'd considered running when he'd gone to help Gil gather wood. But he'd promised Grace to see that Yvette got safely to the Parkers and he didn't mean to disappoint her.

The boys watched them, eyes wide. Tad looked hopeful, but Gil appeared resigned.

"There's no way out," Gil said. "We've looked and looked. Uncle even put logs on the floor. We haven't anything sharp enough to dig through them."

"Does he often leave you here alone?" Sam went to a wall and visually examined every log. He took a dull kitchen knife and jabbed it into each. Everything was solid.

"He leaves us lots," Tad said. "But I'd sooner be

locked in here than with him. He makes us do bad things." Tad turned to Gil. "Mama and Papa would be very disappointed in us."

Gil pulled his little brother to his side, a gesture that reminded Sam of how protective he'd been of Grace when they were about that age. "They'd understand. Like Mama said, when we're in a bad spot we have to pray and trust God to send rescue." He beamed at Sam. "Guess God sent you."

Yvette cleared her throat and gave Sam a look full of challenge.

He ignored her and spoke to the boys. "I don't know if God sent me, but I'll do my best to get us all out of here." He continued circling the room, testing each log. With every foot he moved, his heart turned heavier. This structure was meant to keep small boys in. But it seemed it would have withstood a dozen men trying to escape.

Aware that the others watched him, expecting him to provide rescue, he kept checking the logs. He had done only two walls when they heard a horse approaching.

Tad went to Gil's side. Gil put an arm around his younger brother's shoulders.

Sam ceased his examining of the logs and stood behind the boys

Yvette's hands curled into fists and she stared at the door.

Not wanting her to be alone and vulnerable, he

caught her arm. She shuddered at his touch, but he ignored her response and pulled her to his side. Her arm remained stiff, so he dropped his hand.

Thudding at the door signaled the arrival of someone. Sam figured no one but Blackie knew of the cabin's existence. When he'd followed Gil outside, he'd seen they were in a clearing barely big enough to contain the cabin. As they'd approached the place yesterday, he'd noted that the trail was barely discernable. Blackie didn't mean for anyone to stumble on its location.

The door swung open and Blackie stood in the opening. "Got two rabbits. Gil, take 'em and skin 'em then cook 'em up."

Gil hurried to obey, snatching the animals as he hurried by.

Sam stepped toward the door. "I'll go help him."

"No, ya won't. Less'n you want to wear a big ole hole in yer head." Blackie aimed his gun toward Sam.

"Sam!" The frightened tone of Yvette's voice stopped him every bit as quickly as Blackie's threats.

He turned toward her. Her eyes were wide, her pupils so enlarged there remained only a rim of her hazel irises. He felt a little thrill to think she cared what happened to him.

"Not another gun shot," she whispered, pressing her hands to her ears.

His thrill died as suddenly as it was born. Her concern was for her own sake.

He nodded and moved back to her side. He had no desire to be shot. Or shot at. Nor did he want to frighten Yvette. Or the children. Live or die, he would do his very best to protect them all and, God willing and with His divine help, get them out of here safely.

So he proposed to move slowly so as to not cause Blackie to be overly watchful. He'd appear to be cooperative, all the while watching for the flaw in Blackie's plans. There had to be a flaw. There was always a flaw if one watched closely enough.

Blackie ordered them to make themselves useful.

Sam wasn't sure what they could do in the small space, but the three of them hurried toward the cupboard and opened the doors to examine the contents. Lots of canned beans. A sack that, upon examination, revealed a good supply of dried pea beans. "We might get tired of beans," he murmured. But at least there was food for the boys.

Tad touched several other sacks and said what was in them. "Cornmeal. I like it best. Rice. Gil likes it best." He pointed out the rolled oats, the flour, and the baking powder. "For biscuits, but we don't know how to make them."

Scotty, the cook back at Circle A Ranch, had taught all the boys to make biscuits and bake them in a Dutch oven. "If we're here long enough, I'll teach you."

"That'd be nice."

There were coffee beans, but Sam didn't see any grinder. Did he see canned peaches in the very back?

Gil returned with two rabbits ready to cook.

Sam put water in the biggest pot and took it to the stove. Gil salted the animal like he had done this before and put it into the water.

"Take a long time for it to be really good."

Sam nodded. "Worth waiting for though." He glanced toward Blackie who had stretched out on the cot, his hat pulled low, and looked as if he slept. Sam was not fooled. The man had the hearing and reflexes of a cat.

As if aware Sam looked his way, he shifted. "Ya got nothin' to do but stare?" He swung his feet over the side of the bed and gave Sam a sour look, then shifted his gaze to Yvette and his eyes narrowed to dangerous slits.

Gil watched his uncle. His shoulders tensed and he swallowed hard then grabbed Tad's hand. "Uncle, can we go outside and look for deadfall?"

Blackie studied the two boys. "Remember I'll hunt ya down like a rabid dog if ya try to run off."

Sam's insides curdled at the way the man talked. He could think of a dozen ways to teach the man some kindness, but the truth was, kindness had to be born in a man's heart. It couldn't be forced.

"Yes, Uncle," the boys said in unison.

Blackie opened the door and the pair hurried out.

Sam looked at the open door, the sunshine and escape. He considered the man's eagerness to use his gun. It wouldn't do any of them any good for him to get halfway into the sheltering trees only to die of a gunshot wound. Yet the outdoors beckoned. Being shut up in such small quarters went against the freedom he enjoyed as a cowboy riding for the Circle A.

"I can help them," Sam said and took a step toward the door.

Blackie laughed. "I don't trust ya. Ya was ready to turn against Miss Bellamy. Not 'xactly a noble way to act."

Yvette made a sound that seemed to be in agreement.

Sam shrugged. It was odd to think that Blackie condemned Sam's actions but imprisoned his own kin.

"I returned last time," he pointed out. He'd only been out a few minutes but he'd taken time to study their surroundings. He didn't see the horses. Blackie must have corralled them somewhere else. The trickle of water suggested they were near a creek of some sort.

"Maybe ya was jest plannin' your escape."

Now was not the time to challenge Blackie.

Blackie glanced over his shoulder. "Don't trust ya. You was ready to turn against Miss Bellamy. Yer not a good man." He returned to watching the boys.

Sam slowly turned his gaze toward Yvette and silently tried to send her a message. One that said he wasn't a bad man. He only wanted to find a way to make Blackie let down his guard.

The way her eyebrows rose, he guessed she wasn't seeing what he meant.

The water in the pot boiled over. Yvette made no move to do anything if she even noticed. Sam lifted the lid and set it at an angle.

One of the boys laughed and both Sam and Yvette moved to one of the slits to look out. Tad chased Gil. Sam grinned to see them enjoying themselves. He wanted to say something about their freedom to play but feared it would only make Blackie call the boys in.

He glanced at Yvette. She stared out the opening. As if sensing him watching her, she turned slowly, a strange look on her face.

If he had to guess what he saw, he would say she looked sad, pained even. "Yvette, what's wrong?" he whispered. Blackie had moved to lean against the frame of the door so Sam considered it safe to talk quietly.

She shook her head, but he caught a glisten of tears in her eyes.

He took a step closer, wondering if she saw something he hadn't, or if she'd picked up a splinter in a finger, but she shook her head again and held up a hand to stop him.

His gaze returned to watching out his hole, but he knew what he'd seen. He leaned his elbows on the sill. A long-forgotten emotion surfaced. One he'd almost forgotten. The helplessness he'd felt back at the orphanage when Grace had been denied yet another home because she had an older brother.

Everything he'd done had been to make the situation better for Grace. Even letting Adam write letters for him had been simply and only to make Grace happier in her new life.

There had to be a way to drive that sadness from Yvette's eyes. First and foremost, it meant finding a way to escape this place.

He left the window and walked to the stove. Then back to the window. Stove and window. Stove and window. He would have liked to go to the door and breathe in sunshine and pine trees but didn't want to challenge Blackie.

Another trip to the window, to the cupboard, and to the stove. Slowly his assurance grew. God was with them. God would surely provide an open door for them. He smiled to himself, thinking an open door unguarded by a bully of a man was exactly what they needed.

Sam would be sure to watch for that opening.

Yvette's throat constricted as she watched the boys playing. Such freedom. Unlike the constraints she'd been under all her life. She acknowledged it was a foolish thought. These boys were in a prison and under the care of a cruel man. They didn't deserve that. There must be something they could do. She could do. She wasn't about to trust Sam for anything. Even Blackie saw him for what he was. Dishonest. An opportunist. Yes, he prayed, but was that just because Maude and John had taught him to? From what she'd learned, the older couple who owned the ranch was very faithful about prayer and Bible reading. They even held Sunday services at their home with John leading them in worship from his wheelchair. Yes, Maude and John were good, God-fearing people. That didn't mean all the cowboys at the ranch were the same, despite appearances.

The walls and ceiling of this room seemed to press in on her. The outdoors beckoned with its light and fresh air and the sky high above. Maybe Blackie would let her go outside.

"Would you let me go out for some fresh air?" She spoke in her most conciliatory tone. "I won't run off when I have no idea of where we are."

"Don't mind walkin' with ya."

She shuddered. Walking with him would ruin any fresh air experience she hoped for, but he waved her through the door and followed her.

He stopped to bar the door to keep Sam in. "Ya can walk around the clearin'." He sat on a log against the house and watched her. Not what she had in mind, but far better than having him at her side. The clearing was very small.

Tad and Gil ran to her side then raced away, enjoying their moment in the sun.

She walked the perimeter of the clearing, aware that Blackie's gaze followed her except for the few feet at the back of the house. She paused there and breathed deeply and freely for the first time since she'd walked into the house back at Logan Crossing, expecting to be greeted by the Parkers. Not a grubby man holding a gun. Before she could think to retreat, he'd grabbed her, pressed the gun to her head, and ordered her into the bedroom. He didn't speak but chortled as he tied her up. Touching her in ways that were invasive and painful. Making her feel defiled.

"What do you want?" she'd demanded before he stuffed her mouth with rags.

"Hear ya're a rich girl. Figger yer pa will pay lots to get ya back."

She growled low in her throat which seemed to amuse her captor. *The blessing of the LORD, it maketh rich, and he addeth no sorrow with it.* It was a verse she had learned by heart after Morgan. The Lord's riches did not bring sorrow with them but man's did. *God, I don't care about riches. They have brought me nothing but sorrow. I want freedom. From this man. From the boundaries that constrain me.* Getting free of Blackie was the most important thing right now. If—when—she did, she would build for herself a life different from her present one. It would be a life where she was viewed and valued for her own sake. Not for her family name or her father's money.

She heard approaching footsteps. It would be Blackie coming to see what took her so long and she hurried onward. How long did he intend to keep her there? The idea of a long stay filled her bones with glass. But if that was his plan, she would take advantage of it.

She'd ask to go outside every day and make no move to make him feel he must keep constant watch of her. She'd pretend she was grateful for his generosity. Give him no reason to think she had plans. And when he trusted her, then she'd run.

"'Nough outside," he growled. "In ya go." He slid back the bar and opened the door.

She gave it a moment's study. It was thick. Each end of the slide was blocked so it couldn't be pushed too far. The man certainly knew how to build a prison.

"Come on, boys," he called.

Gil and Tad raced into the house.

Yvette followed, pausing long enough to speak to Blackie. "Thank you for letting me have a walk. I appreciate it."

"Huh." He sounded more suspicious than grateful, but he'd soon begin to trust her. Disregarding her, he bent to lock the door.

Sam's eyes narrowed as he watched her.

She ignored him.

Gil had gone to the stove to check on the rabbit.

She meant to go to his side, but Sam blocked her path.

"Don't be thinking you can sweeten him up to release you. All he wants is the ransom money." His words were barely whispers.

She lifted her head, meeting his eyes with such fierceness he flinched. "Are you saying I should trust you?" There was no way he could miss the scorn in her voice.

"I'm all you've got. I'll help you get—"

"No, I've got my own wits." She edged past him to stand by Gil. "That smells good, Gil."

Tad handed her a dipperful of water. "Did you see the blue flowers by the woodpile?"

"No, I didn't. I'll have to watch for them next time." She glanced from under her lashes to see if Blackie paid any attention. But he was rooting through his saddlebags. Well, Rome wasn't built in a day.

Blackie straightened. "That rabbit cooked?"

"Yes, Uncle." The boys stood back as Blackie approached. He grabbed a battered tin plate from the cupboard and dug out some meat then sat on the cot and ate, completely unconcerned about the others or about manners.

Sam grabbed three bowls and a plate from the cupboard, dug out portions of meat to put on each and handed it to them. "Shall we pray?" he asked.

Yvette slowly bowed her head. How did the way this man prayed over his food in such abhorrent conditions fit with her picture of him choosing the easy, and not always honorable, way?

At his 'amen' she began to eat. "This is good," she said, surprised at its tastiness.

Blackie finished and returned to fiddling with his saddlebags.

Gil and Tad continually sent worried looks at each other, making Yvette's nerves grow tighter and tighter at the tension in their little faces.

Sam watched them too. He looked at Yvette and lifted his brows. She understood his silent message.

The boys knew something was going on with their uncle and it had them on edge.

Their nervousness gripped her. What was the man planning? Whatever it was, it would surely affect her.

Toward evening, they ate some more of the rabbit meat, with rice to accompany it. It wasn't a bad meal, but Yvette had a hard time eating more than a few bites.

Blackie tied his saddlebags closed and put them on the cot, then sat staring at the far wall. He dragged one booted foot closer, the sound shattering any sense of peace in her brain.

She almost dropped her plate of food.

He dragged the other foot closer to the bed and sighed.

The air in the room crackled with tension.

Tad drew in a sharp breath. Gil touched his arm to silence him.

Yvette, wondering at what, other than their uncle, caught their attention, looked around.

A mouse. She lifted a finger and pointed, a squeal climbing up her throat.

Sam curled his hand around hers. "Shh," he whispered and nodded toward the boys who regarded the mouse with more concern than fear. Both of them pressed their lips tight, their eyes wide and made flicking motions toward the mouse.

Yvette gripped Sam's hand and shivered. Mice were sneaky little rodents that raced around, sometimes over one's feet. Even climbing one's stocking. She couldn't breathe for holding back a scream.

Blackie shifted his squinty eyes toward the boys.

They lowered their heads and concentrated on their food, though they didn't lift anything to their mouths.

"Whatcha boys up ta?"

"Nothing, Uncle," Gil said. "I like rice."

"Then why isn't ya eatin' it?"

"I am." Both boys hurriedly took a spoonful and chewed as if it was the best thing they'd ever tasted.

Yvette kept her head down but from under cover of her lashes, she watched the mouse. If it made a move toward her, she wouldn't be able to sit quietly. No. She'd be standing on the chair, screaming.

Blackie, unconvinced of his nephews' innocence, looked around.

She knew the minute he saw the mouse. He was on his feet,

"I'll get that little varmint."

Tad rose as well but Gil caught his hand and held him back.

Blackie stomped, but the mouse was faster and ran under the cot. Blackie yanked the cot from the wall, overturning it. "Where'd ya go, ya little varmint?"

Tad turned to Yvette, his eyes large and glistening with tears. "He's our pet." The words chattered over his teeth.

Yvette didn't care for mice, but even less, she didn't care to see someone's pet hunted. But she could do nothing but squeeze Tad's shoulder. "Maybe he got away."

"Where'd ya go?" Blackie tossed aside pieces of wood. He shook the boys' bedding then tore the blankets from the cot and shook them.

Every time, Yvette shuddered, imagining a mouse thrown in her direction.

But there was no mouse. Even so, Blackie continued to stomp about making dire threats.

Suddenly, he stopped in front of the boys.

"The two of ya hadn't better been feedin' him," he bellowed.

"No, Uncle," Gil said.

Tad swallowed hard but couldn't seem to get a word out.

"I find out ya's been wastin' food on a mouse, y'all

pay." He grabbed both boys by a shoulder and shook them, their heads jerking back and forth. Gil clamped his teeth together, but Tad let out a sob that seemed to further annoy their uncle.

Yvette wanted to catch the man's hands and make him stop.

Why didn't Sam do something to end this torture? What did she expect? Wasn't he the sort of man who always took the easy way out? Look at how he'd let Adam write to Grace, pretending to be Sam. Or how Sam had tried to get into partnership with Blackie.

And he thought she should depend on him to get them out of this predicament?

Well, no thanks. She'd depend on her own wits and God's help.

4

Sam's fingers creaked from the pressure of him balling his fists. Under ordinary circumstances, he would have intervened... used his fists to stop the man if necessary. But with no place for any of them to escape the man's wrath, Sam knew he couldn't do something that would likely make things worse. A bully like Blackie would not quit until he'd punished all of them.

Sam had seen the depths a bully would go to. And he didn't intend to create such a situation.

He must divert the man. Could think of only one way to do it. He went to the turned-over cot and set it to rights.

Blackie stopped shaking the life out of the boys. "Whatcha think yer doin'?"

"Guessing you'd be wanting this bed soon. Figure

to get it ready is all." He spoke slowly; as if his brain didn't function at full speed.

"Huh."

Blackie watched as Sam spread the blankets on the cot, but when he reached for the saddlebags, Blackie shouted.

"Don't be touchin' my things."

Sam lifted his hands, palms toward Blackie to indicate he meant no trouble and backed away, almost stumbling over the boys' blankets scattered on the floor.

Blackie grabbed Gil's ear. "Hey, what's yer blankets doin' all over the floor?"

No one pointed out that Blackie had put them there, though Sam wondered if Yvette was biting her tongue to keep silent. Good thing Blackie wasn't looking at her because her eyes spoke volumes—mainly anger and displeasure.

She shifted her attention to Sam and he drew back at the hardness in her eyes. Did she think he should have stepped in to stop Blackie from abusing the boys? But he knew to confront the man would likely increase his anger and lead to unwanted results. He couldn't smile and flutter his lashes at him like Yvette did, but he could do his best not to rile the man either.

Like now. He thought of helping the boy with the blankets, but the scowl on Blackie's face warned him it would be wise to let Gil do it.

Gil gathered up the blankets and folded them

crookedly before piling them against the wall where they had been.

The job done, he faced his uncle. "Sorry, Uncle."

A protest rose on Sam's mouth, but he kept his lips clamped together and hoped the look he gave Yvette warned her to do the same.

Blackie released Tad. "Clean up the dishes then go to bed." He sank to the cot and pulled his saddlebags close.

What did those bags contain that Blackie was so protective of? Probably his ill-gotten money from robberies and the key to the lock on the door. Sam didn't care about any money, but could he get his hand on the bags after Blackie fell asleep and find the key?

It was certainly worth a try.

Later, the dishes washed and put away, Blackie stretched out on his cot and ordered the others to do the same.

Sam took his time. Every bit of his brain raced with possible ways of escaping this man. Every possibility ran smack into a rock-solid roadblock. Or more accurately, a locked door. If only he could find the key. If he could just get his hands on those saddlebags for a few minutes.

Yvette and Tad chose a spot on the floor.

"What about the mouse?" Yvette asked, shuddering.

Tad patted her arm. "He won't hurt you. If he comes to visit, I'll take him."

Tad was very protective of Yvette. It was good to

see, though the boy would be but an annoying insect to his uncle if there was any sort of confrontation.

As he had done the previous night, Sam positioned himself between Yvette and Blackie. If it came to protecting Yvette from a physical attack by their captor, Sam meant to stand in the way. Even if it cost him his life. He prayed it wouldn't come to that for he'd not be of any help to them if he was dead.

Besides, he did not have any desire to die just yet. Nope, there were things he wanted to do.

He sat with his back to the wall and waited in the darkness.

And waited.

Blackie's breathing deepened.

Sam continued to wait.

Surely the man was sound asleep. Now was the time to act.

Sam moved soundlessly, shifting away from the wall and inching across the floor to the side of the cot. He'd seen Blackie put the saddlebags to his far side and he eased to his knees. He stopped, listening for any sound of Blackie's breathing changing.

Slowly, moving with infinite care, he reached across Blackie's chest and gasped as hands clamped around Sam's throat, squeezing his windpipe until Sam couldn't breathe.

Sam fought to free himself. Blackie's strength surprised him.

Blackie rose from the bed, still holding Sam by the

throat. He backed Sam to the nearest wall and slammed his head into the logs.

Pain and lack of air made things so black Sam wondered if the moon had disappeared.

Blackie released him and he collapsed to the floor, his head pounding like someone hammered nails into it.

"I've a good mind to shoot ya. But it'd be a waste of a bullet. Try any more funny stuff and I'll figger it to be a bullet well spent." Blackie threw himself on the cot.

"Are you all right?" Gil whispered into the silence.

"I've felt better on occasion." Every word, though but a faint whisper, thundered through his head.

"He coulda killed you."

"Guess so." Sam leaned against the wall. But as soon as the bump on the back of his head touched the logs, he sat forward and leaned over his knees. That might have been a dumb thing to do. But then it wasn't the first dumb thing he'd done in his life and wouldn't likely be the last.

"Lie down." Gil pulled him toward the floor.

He lowered himself to the blanket.

"That was either the bravest or the dumbest thing I've ever seen," Yvette whispered close to his ear.

"I know."

Gentle hands pulled a blanket over him and tucked it around his shoulders.

"Go to sleep now." A hand patted him. A gentle hand.

And despite the throbbing in his head, or perhaps *because* of the injury to his head, he slept.

HE WOKE the next morning with a headache the size of an ocean. Even though he didn't want Blackie to know how bad it hurt to move, he guessed from the gleam in the man's eyes and the worried looks on the faces of the others, that he wasn't succeeding in moving the way he normally would. Truth was, it hurt to move and he did so cautiously and slowly.

"Guess that'll learn ya." The man's cackle of glee roared through Sam's head. "Might keep ya out of trouble while I'm gone."

That cleared Sam's head in a hurry. "Where are you going?"

"Gotta get my money." He slung the saddlebags over his shoulders and bent to unlock the door.

"Uncle," Gil spoke with fear and trembling. "Where are you going and when will you be back?"

Blackie straightened and faced his nephew. "To the fort, if'n it's any of yer bizness."

Sam guessed it was the business of all of them.

"There's plenty of food in the cupboard. The bucket is mostly empty. Hope it don't overflow 'for I get back." The way the man grinned said he didn't care if it did. "Adios."

Sam's slow brain said there was something wrong with Blackie's plan, but he couldn't think well enough to know what it was.

Until Blackie stepped out into the sunlight.

Sam sprang forward even though his head protested at the sudden movement. "Hey, there's a slight problem with your plan."

Blackie squinted at Sam. "I got it all figgered out."

"Why would anyone give you money for Miss Bellamy if you don't have her? Seems to me they'll want to get her in exchange for any money they have."

Blackie studied the idea a moment then shook his head. "Nobody getting her less'en I has the money." And with that, he slammed the door. The thud and creak informed them all that the door was soundly and securely barred.

The four of them stared at the barrier and listened to Blackie ride away. Silence as deep as a mining pit filled the room.

Sam tried to think through the situation. But thoughts were reluctant to come. "I could sure use a cup of coffee."

"We got coffee beans," Gil said. "But they're for Uncle."

"Uncle isn't here." Sam put a pot of water on the stove, added a chunk of wood to the fire and then found the coffee beans. He might not be able to grind them properly but he could smash them. In fact, he was about ready to chew them whole if it would drive away his headache.

He put a handful in a not too dirty rag, set it on a piece of log and proceeded to use another hunk of wood to smash the beans. He opened the cloth. Satisfied they were sufficiently crushed, he added the grounds to the hot water and waited for it to boil then poured himself a cupful and offered another to Yvette. At first, she hesitated, then took it with a murmured word of thanks.

The boys watched the adults.

Sam sucked back the brown liquid. "I've tasted better."

Yvette grimaced. "I've never tasted worse."

He grinned. "I'd apologize, but it's the best I can do under the circumstances." His head feeling clearer, he gave the room and its occupants serious study. "So, he's gone. To Fort Macleod, I assume." He wasn't exactly sure where this cabin was but far enough from any sort of civilization that no one would discover it. "I'm going to assume he'll be gone most of a week."

"A week?" Yvette bolted to her feet. "We'll di—" Her gaze lit on the boys and she swallowed back whatever she'd been about to say. She turned toward Sam. "That long?"

Sam nodded, wishing he could erase the fear in her eyes. "That gives us several days to find a way out of here."

"There isn't any," Gil said.

"Then we'll make a way."

"How?" Defeat showed in Gil's expression and the way his shoulders slumped.

"I don't know." Sam drained his cup and began an inspection of each log again. But he found no weakness. The man certainly knew how to build well.

He finished inspecting the walls. Though the last wall got barely a glance. He faced the expectant look on Yvette's face and the resignation on the boys'.

Her gaze went to the bucket. He guessed she needed to use it but, like himself, found it almost unbearable to do so in plain view of the others. That was something he could fix. To a degree. He snagged up a blanket off the floor and using his knife and some wood wedges, fixed it to the ceiling, then stood back.

"It provides a degree of privacy."

Yvette's gaze went from Sam to the curtain and back again.

He couldn't say what she was thinking except to know she was surprised. He hoped her surprise was laced with gratitude.

Gil had made cornmeal mush. The others had eaten while Sam explored. Gil handed him a bowl of the food.

Sam sat on the chair and ate, his thoughts going round and round. He remembered something, his spoon halfway to his mouth. "The mouse."

Yvette had returned and snorted. "What are you

going to do? Tie a note to him and order it to go to the nearest abode?"

"Well, if I thought I could trust a mouse…" He shook his head and instantly regretted it. The movement reminded him of his bruised skull. "But the mouse must be getting in somewhere." He pulled the cot from the wall and got down on his hands and knees. "Yes, see. There's a hole here."

Yvette stood beside him, her arms crossed. "Too bad we're all bigger than a mouse."

"The log here must be softer." Sam took out his pocketknife and began to dig at the hole.

Yvette sat on the side of the cot, watching. The boys squatted at his elbows.

After a couple minutes Sam decided the mouse must have found the only soft spot in the log. He could barely scrape away any of the wood. Nevertheless, it was the best escape route he'd found so far.

Sometime later, he paused to rest his muscles and sat beside Yvette on the cot.

The boys studied the progress he'd made. Gil shook his head. "Can't even get my hand through it." He took Tad's hand and led him away. All of ten feet to the stove.

"It's hopeless, isn't it?" Yvette whispered.

"I'm not about to admit defeat." He looked to where the boys were. They sat cross-legged on the floor, facing each other and played with some pieces of wood. "Look at them. The only toys they have are bits of wood. They have no freedom. How often do you think Blackie leaves them shut in here?" His words lowered to a growl. "They shouldn't have to live this way."

"I couldn't agree more." After a moment, she sighed. "But what are we to do about it?"

We? She'd said we? "Are you starting to see me as more friend than foe?"

A tiny smile curved her mouth. "Seems we're in this together."

"There has to be a way out. Gil, what did you use to skin the rabbits?"

"Uncle has a knife he lets me use."

"Where does he keep it?"

"I don't know. Somewhere outside. I've watched him, but he never puts it away when I'm around. I've looked for it when he didn't know I was. Never seen it."

Sam discarded that possibility. "He must have an ax for chopping wood."

Gil nodded. "He keeps it under the doorway. I once tried to get it when he wasn't looking, but he caught me." The way Gil's voice dropped, Sam guessed the boy had been punished cruelly.

Tad looked from Gil to Sam and Yvette. "Uncle beat him." The younger boy's voice shook.

"Oh Gil." Yvette opened her arms. "I'm sorry. Come here and I'll give you a hug. You too, Tad."

The boys hesitated then slowly crossed to Yvette as

she motioned them forward. She pulled them into her arms and held them tight. Inch by inch, they relaxed against her. Tad let out a soft sigh.

Yvette looked up at Sam, her eyes awash in unshed tears. "Isn't there something we can do about their situation?"

"Only if we can get away from here."

She stroked two little heads. The boys were thin. Their light brown hair was shaggy. Two little waifs in need of love. "Why didn't he take you to an orphanage?" she asked.

Gil sniffled. "He meant to, but then he saw how people would talk to us so he could rob them."

"Mama and Papa would be so sad at what we've done," Tad whispered. It was an idea that obviously weighed heavily on the child's mind.

Yvette's arms tightened around the boys and she pressed her cheek to their heads. "They would be sad but not at what you've done. They'd only be sad and angry at how your uncle treats you." She gave Sam a pleading look. "We have to get out of here. Get away from that man."

He held her gaze and nodded. "We just have to figure out how."

"If someone could get out and get that ax."

"Someone small."

Tad straightened. "I could do it."

"Of course you could. We just have to find or make a hole big enough for you." He pushed on the roof.

Solid as a rock. His gaze went to the window slots. It might be their best option. "We'll widen one enough for Tad to get out."

But an hour later, he admitted it would take more than a week to make a large enough opening for anyone to escape. If only he had something bigger than his little pocketknife that was getting duller by the minute.

He stepped back, realized that Yvette and the boys watched him. They wore expectant expressions. He folded the blade back into the knife and shook his head. "This isn't going to work."

"It has to." Yvette grabbed his knife, opened the blade and tackled the logs.

Sam waited with the boys. In a few minutes she stepped back. "You're right. It's hopeless." She sank to the cot with an air of dejection.

"What're we going to do?" Gil whispered.

Sam looked around at the little circle of those imprisoned with him. A sense of failure engulfed him. There had to be something he could do to make things better for all of them. He shifted his gaze to the interior of the cabin. Barring a miracle, there didn't appear to be any way out. His gaze lit on the stove. They could burn the place down. He quickly dismissed that idea. With no way of escape, they would burn to death.

But there was one thing he could do.

"I'll teach you all how to make biscuits. Tad, you

get a big bowl. Gil, you get that cast iron fry pan and put it on the stove." The boys hurried to do his bidding. "Yvette?" He wasn't about to order her around.

She rose slowly, a half expectant, half doubtful look on her face. "You could teach me to cook?" She ducked her head. "I don't know how."

He held back his reaction that in his opinion everyone should know the basics. "Scotty insisted we all learn enough to get by. He said it was so he didn't have to go out with us any longer." He chuckled softly. "I wonder if it wouldn't have been easier for him to run the chuckwagon than to teach a bunch of boys how to cook." He held out a hand to Yvette. "Come on, I'll show you how to make biscuits." He pulled her to her feet and drew her toward the cupboard where he instructed them on measuring the flour and baking soda. There was a container of lard in the corner and he had Yvette mix it in with her fingers. Laughed when she said it was fun.

"Just enough water to make a soft dough." Yvette slowly added water.

"Good. Perfect." He divided the dough into three and let each of them knead it and cut it into circles. "Now you grease the hot fry pan and put biscuits in it. Got to watch them closely." All of them fit into the pan. He covered it with a tin plate. "Now we wait."

Yvette opened the cupboard. "What else can I make?"

"Beans." He looked over her shoulder. "Pancakes." He moved a few cans of beans. "Peaches. I think you could make a cobbler. All you have to do is make biscuits to go on top of the peaches. But we'll have to ration the food. So biscuits today with the leftover rabbit and rice."

She turned to smile up at him. "I have always wanted to learn how to cook."

"So, why didn't you?" Seemed to him a rich girl could pay someone to teach her almost anything she wanted.

Her smile disappeared, replaced with a faraway look in her eyes. "My parents didn't consider it appropriate for me to be in the kitchen."

He chuckled. "I don't suppose they thought you'd learn to cook a few things in a situation like this."

She moved to look out the window slot. "I might never see my parents again."

"Come. I'll show you how to turn the biscuits over to brown the top."

When they were done, he let Gil lift them onto a plate.

"Those look delicious," Sam said.

"Can we eat now?" Tad swallowed audibly.

Before Sam could answer, a thump on the door drew all eyes in that direction.

Had Blackie changed his mind and returned?

Sam's gaze slid toward the place in the window frame where he'd whittled at the logs.

Would Blackie notice? What would his reaction be?

Yvette's breath burned up and down her throat. If that vile man had returned, what did it mean? She'd sooner die in this prison than become a victim of his evil actions.

He banged on the door again. A thud rather than a knock. Though why would he knock?

Another thud.

Her heart clawed at her throat. Beating insistently. Demandingly. Telling her to run. Hide. But there was nowhere to run and no place to hide.

"Why isn't he coming in?" Gil's whisper was almost a groan.

Sam answered. "Maybe he's injured."

"We can't help him." Not that they wanted to except to be set free.

The sound moved away from the door. A snuffling, whoofing sound informed them he made his way around the cabin. Perhaps to look in the narrow windows.

Yvette's gaze followed the sound.

A big brown head appeared in the slot. Or least part of what they could see of it through the opening.

She squealed.

Sam caught her hand and squeezed. "It's a bear. He can't get in."

The animal pressed his nose to the opening and sniffed. He scratched at the logs.

Gil and Tad pressed to the adults. Sam wrapped an arm over the boys, holding them close.

Yvette edged closer but resisted the urge to lean fully on Sam.

"He can't get in," Sam repeated. "But it gives me an idea." He eased himself away from the boys and Yvette's grip and went to the cupboard, spooned out a dollop of lard and put it on the log near where the bear's nose was. Just out of reach of the hungry tongue. He returned to Yvette's side.

She meant to be strong and independent. Just not at this moment. And she held his hand with every ounce of strength she had which, she realized, was mostly nerves and quaking at the moment.

"I'm hoping he'll claw at the logs trying to get the lard. Maybe he'll make a hole large enough for someone to get out and get us that ax."

"But the bear..." She didn't finish. Everyone knew the bear was there. Crawling out a hole in the wall only made a person look like bear food.

"Eventually, he'll give up and go away," Sam said.

She wondered if he was aware of the uncertainty in his voice. "When?" She'd like a little more assurance than that.

"When he gets tired of trying to get the lard."

For some reason, his simple answer amused her and she laughed.

Three pairs of eyes turned toward her.

She stilled her laughter but could feel it pouring from her eyes. "I guess the tension of the past few days has caught up with me. Who'd ever think I'd be locked up in a jail?" She waved her arm around to indicate the interior of the cabin. "Hoping to be freed by a bear who would probably just as soon eat me as let me go?" Laughter engulfed her, ringing from the rafters and bouncing off the walls.

The bear whoofed and disappeared.

Whoops. She'd brought a stop to their only hope of escape, but she still couldn't stop laughing.

The boys laughed too and hopped up and down.

Sam crossed his arms over his chest and studied her. His eyes were watchful. She guessed he thought she might have lost her mind.

"I'm..." She fluttered a hand at him, wanting to tell him she was fine, but all that came out was more laughing.

He grinned. Gave a little chuckle. But he still watched her like he wondered if she might suddenly start screaming. The thought made her laugh even harder.

"I'm fine," she finally gasped.

"You're certain about that?"

Feeling playful, she caught his hands and danced around the room, dragging him lead-footed after her. "I'm better than fine."

They stopped at the stove. Her stomach growled. "I'd like to try our biscuits. Boys, what do you think?"

They were at her side in a heartbeat. "Yes," they said in unison.

Looking slightly bewildered by this change in her, Sam dished up rabbit and rice and handed them each two biscuits. They sat in a circle on the floor.

"Not bad," she said after the first bite of a biscuit she'd made. "Sure could use some butter though."

"Mama used to make butter."

Tad's words sobered Yvette. But only momentarily. "Let's play a game. Why don't we each tell things about our families? I'll start." If they had to perish here, she intended they would go laughing until the end. Or at least smiling. And holding hands to reassure each other. Strange how she could view Sam as a man who took the easy way out and yet find strength in his presence in this prison. The way she'd clung to his hand a short time ago proved just how much she did so.

There wasn't any point in trying to understand it.

She wanted this to be a way of encouraging all of them, so she searched her memories for something uplifting. "I remember when a girl about my age was adopted by our good friends, the Munroes." She was careful to speak to the boys, though she wondered what Sam would think of her friendship with Grace.

"What's adopted?" Tad asked.

"That's when a child whose parents have died is

taken into another family and is forever their child now."

"You can do that?" Tad looked from Yvette to Sam. They both nodded. "Anyone can 'dopt you?"

"Most anyone," she said, and wondered at the look that passed between the two boys. "Let me continue with my story. I was raised in a very strict home. I had to behave a certain way. Walk. Not run. Sit quietly. Never be noisy. Read. Not chase." She sighed at the memory. "But when Grace came I found out not everyone had to live by those rules. She loved to chase and run and laugh out loud. When I was with her, I felt like I'd found freedom."

"You must miss her a lot," Sam murmured, pressing his hand to hers.

"I do, but I have plans for a way to find my freedom again." Not that she could fulfill those plans unless she got out of this place.

"Who's next?" she asked before Sam could question her on what she thought she'd do for the sake of her freedom.

"Me," the boys both spoke at once.

"You go first," Gil said.

Tad leaned forward eagerly. "When I was little, Mama would sing me to sleep. Sometimes I sing to myself now, but it's her voice I pretend I hear." He scrubbed at his eyes.

Yvette reached over to squeeze his shoulder at the

same time as Sam and his hand pressed against hers. Warm and solid.

She withdrew. This was the man who would do whatever was to his advantage. But who also affixed a curtain around the odorous bucket and also taught a rich girl and two little boys to bake biscuits. Who'd tried to find a way of escape and paid for it with a blow to his head.

She shepherded her thoughts back to where they belonged. "That was very nice Tad. Gil, do you want to be next?"

He nodded and cleared his throat. "Papa was a strong man. I remember how he would hold out his arm like this." He held out an arm horizontally. "I would wrap my hands around his fist and he would carry me across the floor. I always let go before he lowered his arm." He turned to Tad. "He was very strong. Remember?"

"I 'member."

Such sweet memories. "Sam's turn."

He got a distant look in his eyes. "Boys, like you, my parents had died. Me and my sister, Grace—"

At the questioning look in Gil's eyes, Sam nodded. "Yes, the girl who is Yvette's friend. Anyway, I knew she would be adopted if she didn't have a big brother so I began to look for work away from the orphanage. About that time, Maude showed up." He explained that Maude was the wife of John Arbuckle. "John had been hurt in an accident and couldn't walk anymore.

Maude could run the ranch, but she needed cowboys. The older men refused to work for her, so she went in search of boys she could train. She found Dillon, Noah, and Adam and signed them on. But she needed more, so she went to the orphanage near Fort Calgary. Pete was a good strong boy. She took him. Mike was big enough too. When I saw what she was doing, I begged for her to take me. I was only thirteen and not full grown yet, but she let me go with her. I've been riding for the Circle A Ranch since that day. Best thing that could have happened to me."

Gil stared at him. "She adopted six of you?"

"We aren't adopted, but we couldn't be any more of a family if we'd been born to them."

"Wish someone would adopt us," Tad whispered.

"First, we'd have to get away from Uncle." Gil made it sound like an impossibility.

Yvette glanced around the room. It seemed an impossibility for any of them to escape.

And what if Blackie took his money and never returned?

Her heart gave a frightened lurch.

They would all die here.

5

Sam was instantly aware of Yvette's changed mood. He didn't have to be very smart to know she wondered if they would ever escape this place. He wished he could offer reassurance that they would, but he shared her concern. The best he could do would be to keep them all entertained and happy.

They finished eating. Gil gathered up the dishes and took them to the little cupboard. Like someone who'd done this many times before, he poured hot water from the pot on the stove and washed the dishes, handing them to Tad to dry.

Sam sat beside Yvette and watched. He moved to the door, hoping Yvette would join him.

She did so. "I don't see any way of getting out of here," she murmured.

"We could use a miracle." He looked into her eyes. He'd thought they were plain hazel but realized they were a stunning mixture of green and gold and brown. Why had he not noticed this before? And at the moment, they were filled with hope and desperation.

He had nothing to offer her in the way of hope but neither could he leave her to wallow in desperation. He took her hands. "We're both God-fearing people. He's a God of miracles. Remember how He made a way through the Red Sea?"

"So we're depending on a miracle?"

He pressed his thumbs to the backs of her hands. "Whether we live or die, God is with us. Let's pray for rescue." He didn't wait for her response but bowed his head and asked God in His great mercy to rescue them. "Amen. In the meantime, we have a task to make those two happy." He tipped his head toward the boys.

"I agree." She didn't turn to look at them. Her gaze remained on him and he looked into her eyes. A silent message passed between them. A wordless vow that made her eyes more green than brown.

"Do you have any suggestions?" she asked.

"We can tell stories, play games…let's do whatever we can under the circumstances."

"I know a game we can play in these small quarters." She turned to the pair who watched them, no doubt wondering what the adults were planning. "Boys, I'm going to teach you a game my nanny taught me when I was sick in bed one time. Let's all sit on the cot."

Yvette sat on one end, Sam at the other with the boys between them while she explained the game.

He put an arm around the boys just as Yvette did the same thing. His arm pressed to her and he looked at her. She stared at him, her eyes brimming with determination.

And maybe a hint of pleasure?

Because of her fondness for the boys? Except she didn't look at them, she looked at him. Her gaze felt like approval. Could that be possible?

Before he could decide if that was what he was seeing, she spoke.

He blinked and righted his thoughts. The only thing that had changed between them was the circumstances and he would remember that. He listened to her instructions for the game they were to play.

"In this game, I pretend to be small. Like a fly. That gives me plenty of places to hide. Then you guess where I am. Shall we try it?"

The boys nodded, faces filled with eagerness at the idea.

"I'm hiding." She sat with her hands folded in her lap, staring straight ahead.

He grinned. She wasn't about to give any clues by looking at the spot.

Sam and the boys guessed places. She guided them by saying warm, hot, or cold. Eventually, Gil found her on the brim of Sam's hat by the door.

They played the game for some time, often

breaking into laughter at some of the places that were used for hiding. Yvette hooted when she 'found' Sam pretending to be in the mouse's hole.

"While you're there, run and fetch the ax," she said.

The boys didn't want to play anymore after that and moved away to get a drink of water.

"I'm sorry," she said to Sam. "That wasn't a good thing to say."

"But it was a good game."

"Thanks." She cocked her head and grinned. "Your turn to come up with something."

He grinned back. "You think I can't, don't you?"

"I'm just curious as to what you'll suggest."

For a moment, he couldn't remember what they were talking about as he watched how her smile made her eyes brighten, and how her expression seemed to suggest fun and games.

Games. That was it.

"Boys, have you ever played statues?"

Gil said he had, but Tad couldn't remember, so Sam explained the rules. "I'll be It. When my back is to you, you can move forward. But if I turn, you have to stand perfectly still, even if your foot is in the air. If I see you move, you go back to the wall. But if you can make it to me, you take my place. Because the room is so small, you can only take baby steps."

Again, they played for a long time and laughed with abandon.

Soon the slanting rays coming through the

windows indicated the day was passing. They ate the last of the rabbit stew and rice.

"We'll need something for tomorrow," Sam said. "Yvette, would you like to learn how to make baked beans? The staple of pioneer and cowboy life."

"Of course. One can never know when it might be important to know such things."

Although her voice seemed airy, he wondered if she considered it a useless skill. After all, if—when—they got out of here, she would return to her rich way of life. Why would she need to know how to bake beans?

But they had to eat and he showed her how to soak the beans. "Then we cook them in the morning." He spoke quietly. "I am not giving up trusting God for a miracle."

The boys sat on the cot, watching them, their shoulders slumped.

"Do you know any stories to tell them?" Sam asked.

"Better than that. I can read to them." She went to one of her valises and removed a Bible. Seeing his surprise, she explained, "I didn't show any interest in my things while Blackie was here. I thought he'd take them if I did."

She was probably right.

"Come on boys. I'm going to read to you." She sat on the cot and patted the spot on either side of her.

"Mama and Papa used to read the Bible to us," Gil said. "And they prayed for Uncle. Mama said he needed to bow the knee to God. What did that mean?"

Sam remained by the cupboard waiting for Yvette to answer.

"I suppose it means choosing to do things God's way rather than our own because we know God is bigger, wiser, and kinder than we can imagine."

"But Uncle doesn't believe in God." Gil seemed confused.

"God has ways of making people see Him and believe in Him. But He doesn't force any of us to believe in Him."

"How does He make people see Him?" Gil asked.

Tad listened carefully to the conversation.

"Let me read you a story and see if you can learn how God shows Himself." She opened the pages. "This is the story of three Hebrew children who refused to worship any other god." She read the story of the three men thrown into the fiery furnace for their refusal and how a fourth man appeared with them and not a hair of their heads was singed.

"That was God showing Himself, wasn't it?" Tad said.

"It was. But He doesn't always show Himself in such miraculous ways. Remember that the men said that their God was able to deliver them but even if He didn't, they wouldn't serve any other god."

The boys looked thoughtful.

Yvette turned the pages. "I'll read you another

story. This one is about sheep and the shepherd. Psalm Twenty-three." She began to read, but Gil held up his hand.

"We can say that." The two boys stood facing her, hands clasped together and recited the entire Psalm.

"Your parents would be so pleased," Yvette's words seemed teary.

Gil turned to Tad. "Remember what Papa said? That the Good Shepherd would be with us always." He looked around the shadowed room. "Even here." He took Tad's hand and led him to the blankets. They spread out a couple and lay down. Gil put his arm around his little brother.

Sam sat on the cot beside Yvette. As she closed her Bible, a bit of paper fell to the floor. He picked it up. It was a clipping from a newspaper. The headline caught his eye.

Seeking Matrimony

Below the headline was several ads of men in the west wanting to meet young women with a view to marriage.

One little square was circled.

He studied it a moment as the truth of what it meant reached his brain. It seemed she meant to seek a mail-order marriage. Why?

"You dropped this." He handed her the clipping.

She took it and stuck it back in her Bible.

"Does this mean what I think it does?" he asked.

Sam

Yvette hadn't intended he should see the ad. But what difference did it make? Like he said, unless God sent a miracle, they were stuck here. Until Blackie returned. *If* he returned. She couldn't help but think of all the things that could happen to him to prevent him from coming back. Accidents like falling down a cliff, breaking a leg...she had no trouble thinking of a dozen things that might befall him. Or someone taking offense to his behavior and shooting him. Besides, why would he bother to return if Father paid the ransom money? He could simply move on.

"I guess there's no harm in telling you I plan to write this man."

"With a view to marriage?"

"You needn't sound so surprised. Lots of women do that."

He studied her, but she kept her attention on the Bible in her lap.

"Women who are desperate, widowed, or have a baby out of wedlock. You have no reason to be desperate."

She gave a tiny snort. "Easy for you to say. You don't know what it's like to be the daughter of a rich man." She raised her eyes to his, heat stinging them. "Do you think I would have been kidnapped if my father was poor? And this isn't the first time I've been used because of it."

"You told me about your ex-beau. I'm sorry. But not all men are out to befriend you because they hope to benefit."

Yvette squirmed around so she faced him fully. "Morgan wasn't the first person to pretend to be my friend simply so they could speak to my father. But it was the worst. I truly believed he cared until the day I overheard him talking to a stranger in the garden. The man was threatening Morgan. Said he'd given him lots of time to pay off what he owed. Morgan said once he persuaded me to marry him, my family would pay his debts. I was shocked and hurt to learn he only cared about me because of my father's money. Money is a burden."

"Some would see it as a blessing. It can be used to do a lot of good. Or it can be the cause of evil." His gaze went to the pair of boys sleeping on the floor. "How does writing to a stranger change any of that?"

"I wouldn't tell him about my father. If we were suitable it would be based on him liking me for myself."

Sam's gaze slowly returned to hers. She told herself she didn't see surprise and even condemnation in that look. Nor was her own heart condemning her.

"So you intend to write letters under false pretenses?"

The question sat like a lump of coal suspended in the air between them.

She didn't answer. Nor did she lower her gaze. "A person must do what they must do."

"How is that any different from me getting Adam to write letters for me?"

"It's different. Besides, I would tell the truth after he learned to care for me."

He pushed to his feet and went to stare out the narrow window. He didn't say anything.

She ran her fingers over the cover of her Bible. What she planned to do wasn't dishonest. Not really. She could justify her reasons. They weren't simply for convenience.

"I have to make sure someone cares about me without the added knowledge of my father's money."

Sam turned from the window but stood with his back against the wall. "Maude says in First Corinthians Thirteen that when it says charity it's a form of love. The chapter says charity rejoices in the truth. I wish I had told Grace the truth a long time ago. My motives were good. I wanted to encourage her. But love deserves the truth. Yvette, how can you build a lasting relationship without honesty?"

His words stung. "I would tell him the truth."

"But the foundation would be full of deceptions. You are who you are. You need a man who can see you for who you are. Not for who your father is."

"That's what I'm seeking."

"I recall something you said to me not very long

ago. You said, 'Truth is truth. Honesty is honesty. Anything else is despicable.'"

"You remember that?" She hadn't expected him to give her words any weight. Her view of this man had been slowly shifting from the time Blackie had abducted her. She'd thought him self-seeking, but he showed real concern for the well-being of the boys. And her? She wasn't sure she was ready to believe so. She knew how desperate her heart was for acceptance and how that made her vulnerable to any acts of kindness. One thing she'd learned was to guard her heart. "Anyway, it's not the same." He too accurately pointed out the flaw in her plan. "I don't intend to deceive, just withhold a portion of the truth until I can trust his feelings."

His expression didn't soften and she guessed he hadn't changed his opinion.

"I don't want to talk about it any longer."

She scanned the room, looking for something else to talk about. Her gaze circled to the sleeping boys. "They'd be better off in an orphanage than with that man."

"Maybe. Maybe not."

Hearing the dark tone of his voice, she looked at him. His face was shadowed, so she couldn't see his expression. "What was it like?"

For several heartbeats, he didn't speak and when he did, his words were so soft she moved to his side to hear him better.

"There were good people there. But also people who weren't good. There was a barn where two milk cows and several horses were cared for. One of my jobs was to milk the cows and help feed them. A man helped out at the orphanage doing outside tasks. He supervised the barn chores. He was a bully who took great delight in making life miserable for those who helped him."

He grew quiet. Was he not going to provide a few details?

"What did he do?"

"Stuff. Just stuff."

"I'm sorry. I don't know what you mean."

He shifted, as if uncomfortable in his own skin. "He'd wait until I was almost done milking, then kick the bucket knowing if I went inside with the explanation that I'd spilled the milk, I'd be whipped."

She gasped.

He held up a hand. "Worse than that was knowing the children, especially the babies, would do without." He rubbed his hand over his forehead. "The man would leave a pile of manure where he knew I would accidentally step in it. A couple times he tripped me and gave a little push so I went face down into a pile of steaming manure." Sam's voice creaked. "I learned not to challenge a bully or try and defend someone else against his attacks. It only makes things worse."

Yvette's heart squeezed out a painful beat. Why must people be so cruel and unfair? Especially to children? She pressed her palm to his bicep hoping he would understand her desire to comfort him.

Sam continued. It seemed that once he began talking, he couldn't stop. He told of so many cruel things the man had done to him that Yvette could hardly bear it.

Finally, he stopped, his breathing raspy. "Sorry, to dump all that on you. It's not something I've ever talked about."

"I'm glad you did. It makes me understand you a little better."

"What do you think you understand?"

She ignored the challenging tone of his question. "I know why you didn't stand up to Blackie. You knew it would make things worse for us. I know why you do your best to make life easier for others. It's how you make up for the bad things you couldn't stop back there. And I know this. Sam, your experiences have taught you how to be kind to others." She exerted a little more pressure of her hand on his arm and felt his muscle twitch beneath her palm.

Neither of them moved. Neither of them spoke and yet she felt a warmth surrounding them. As if learning about his past had erased the tension between them that had been built on her judgment of his fake letter writing. He was right, she couldn't condemn him when she was about to do something similar. But what had really changed between them was her view of him as a suffering boy who had grown into a kind man.

He was the first to move. "It's late. We better get some sleep. No telling what the morrow holds. You can have the cot. I'll sleep by the boys."

She followed him across the room. He lay down on the floor, Gil on one side and Tad on his other. She stretched out on the cot, trying not to think of Blackie having slept there so recently. Though she couldn't ignore the scent of his body beneath her cheek. She shifted, seeking a place that didn't carry that odor. She moved again. And again, but failed to find such a place and flipped to her back, knowing she wouldn't likely sleep.

Sam shuffled to the side of the cot and sat with his back to the thin mattress. "Can't sleep?"

"No. Am I keeping you awake?"

"Couldn't sleep either. What's keeping you awake besides the obvious that we are locked up here wondering if we'll ever get free?"

"We'll get free. And when we do, I'm going to get custody of those boys." She didn't know how, but there had to be a way. Her father would help her find it.

"And do what with them? Besides, I figured to take them to the Circle A. I could be their guardian. They'd get lots of care from everyone and would grow up in the west."

"Don't they need more than that?" she insisted.

"Like what?"

"A family? I could give them that." It wasn't the worst reason in the world for marriage.

"You mean the man you're planning to write to? Does he say two children welcome?"

"He'd have to agree."

"One small flaw in your plan. Their uncle is next of kin. Can't fight that."

"My father will hire the best lawyer. I'll get them somehow."

"So there are times it's good to have a rich father?"

"Maybe. Like you said, money can be used for good."

Silence followed her statement. Had he fallen asleep? Or had she said something to offend him? She reviewed their conversation. Letter writing, bullies, orphans—all of which were potential sore spots for him. But the latest topic had been about orphans.

"I talk like I regret the parents I have. That is not so. I only wish people would see me as me. Not Miss Bellamy. I love my parents and am grateful for the home I have." Even if she longed for a home of her own where she would be loved with abandon. "It's unkind of me to seem so unhappy about my situation when you were orphaned." In the silvery moonlight, she found his shoulder and pressed her hand to it. "I'm sorry for all that you've endured."

Still more silence.

She felt his shoulder rise and fall as if he'd only now remembered to breathe.

"Maude and John have taught us boys so much about God."

His voice was so low that she moved closer to the edge of the cot, her face close to his head.

"They often repeat a verse. 'And we know that all things work together for good to them that love God.'"

She waited, but he didn't explain what he meant.

"Sam, have things worked out for good in your life? Present circumstances not taken into account?"

His chuckle surprised her. "I was hurt and disappointed when my parents died. At their passing, of course. Grace and I knew they were very sick. The preacher's wife stayed with them that last night. The preacher came to visit after dark and spoke to his wife, then they told us Mama and Papa had gone to heaven. The next morning friends called. Mama and Papa were buried. We were homeless. My best friend, Bertie Brown, stood beside me. Grace clung to my hand. I asked Bertie if we could go home with him. If we could live with him. His mother said we could stay a few nights, but other arrangements would have to be made. A few days later, they took us to the orphanage. We were just two small children. How hard would it be for them to keep us? But the parents said if I'd been a little older. If Grace was old enough to help but as we weren't..." His words trailed off into the darkness of the room.

And—she guessed—into the even deeper darkness of his memories.

"I guess that's when I first realized I wasn't good enough."

If she hadn't been leaning so close, she wouldn't have heard the whispered words that ripped through her heart.

"Sam, I'm sorry." He wasn't that different from her. They both sought someone who would see them for who they were.

But who was this cowboy? The man who'd deceived his sister? Who, in her opinion, took the easy road through life? Or the man who went out of his way to make this prison a little more bearable?

6

Sam moved away from the bed, prepared to stretch out by the boys. What was wrong with him to confess something like that to Yvette? Before now, he hadn't even acknowledged the thought to himself.

Before he'd put six inches between him and Yvette, he changed his mind and returned to the spot at her side.

"Forget I said that."

She didn't answer. Had she fallen asleep?

Then her hand returned to his shoulder—a warm comfort. "Are you denying its truth?"

He wanted to. He needed to. But he couldn't find the words. With her hand on his shoulder and the two of them in the pale moonlight that edged through the window openings, it felt safe to express the thoughts that had dogged him a good portion of his existence.

He'd hidden his feelings well, even from himself. They were but a dark shadow in contrast to the sunshine and light of most of his life.

"Being a cowboy is what I am. I enjoy tending the cows, training the horses, riding the range. Maude and John are good and kind."

"I saw that while I was there even if I hadn't learned it from the letters to Grace."

She was kind enough not to remind him that Grace thought the letters came from him.

He continued, wanting her to see that he was happy with his lot. "If I couldn't have my own parents, I couldn't have asked for better than John and Maude. They patiently taught us all how to be cowboys." He shifted, wanting to look into her face as he talked. He blinked to see how close she was. No wonder it had felt like her breath brushed across his cheek. "They made us into a family. They did so many special things."

"Tell me." She smiled, her teeth gleaming in the moonlight. A strand of her brown hair had fallen across her cheek and, without thinking, he lifted it, his fingers brushing the warm softness of her skin. He moved the hair back and slowly withdrew his hand though, if he had had the right, he would have stroked her cheek. Run his finger along her jawline to her ear and back to her chin. And if he was very bold, up to her full pink lips.

He swallowed hard and reminded himself she wanted to hear about life on the ranch.

He told her about learning to ride and rope. "To this day I can't figure out why Maude didn't give up on me. Have you ever tried to make a rope hold a loop while you swing it and then have that loop land over the head of a running animal?" He laughed at his question. "Of course you haven't. Nor had I until then. Pa was a carpenter and bricklayer. He only rode a horse to go places. But Maude knew I had to learn if I was to work on the ranch. She'd show me. I'd try and fail. She'd show me again. Oh, how I wanted to get it right." He jerked his head back.

"I just remembered something. Maude said I expected to fail and as long as I did, I would. 'Expect to succeed and you'll do much better,' she said. 'After all. It's only a length of jute. It doesn't have a mind or a will. But you do.' Guess she was right because shortly after that, I learned how to swing a loop and put it over a cow's head."

"Maude's the first woman I've known who is also a cowboy. Or do you say cowgirl?"

"I understand she rode side by side with John when they started out. He's always said she was better at roping than he was. After John was hurt, she had to do it on her own while worrying about John, whether he'd recover or not."

"She's one strong woman." Yvette sighed. "She makes city life look pampered."

No amount of money or persuasion would convince Sam to confess he'd often thought the same. In fact, he'd half-expected Yvette to whimper and cry about the way Blackie had treated her.

"I wonder if I could be as strong as she is."

Sam heard the wistful tone of her words. And understood something about her. Her life had prevented her from becoming all she could be or wanted to be. "I hope you don't have to go through what she did to believe you can. But in a way, you already have. Did you break down when Blackie tied you so cruelly? Have you curled into a defeated ball at being imprisoned like this? No. I think you are made of stronger stuff than you realize." He prayed her strength wouldn't be challenged in worse ways.

"Thank you for saying that." She reached out her hand and he took it and squeezed. "It's easy to be brave when you're here."

"I'm happy if I help."

Their gazes held across the few inches between them. No words were spoken. None were necessary. They were in this together and they would live or die side by side. Along with two innocent children.

He cupped his free hand over hers, sandwiching her hand between his. "Come what may, we will be a team."

"I am stronger already. But we still need a miracle."

"God willing."

He held tightly to her hand. Unless Blackie

returned, or God intervened, they would die in this place.

She put her hand on top of his. "Whatever happens, we are together in this."

They clung to each other and their determination for several minutes.

"You need to get some sleep," he said, reluctantly withdrawing his hands.

"I'll try." She moved closer to the middle of the narrow cot and closed her eyes. "You need sleep too."

"I'll try," he echoed softly. Before he shifted away, he rested his hand on her forehead. "'The Lord bless thee, and keep thee: The Lord make his face shine upon thee, and be gracious unto thee: The Lord lift up his countenance upon thee and give thee peace.'"

She opened her eyes and caught his hand, keeping it on her forehead. "Thank you and God be with you too."

For a heartbeat…two…three he didn't move. The moment felt almost holy. Full of tenderness. Promising something that he longed for but couldn't quite grasp.

"Good night." He slipped away to lie beside the boys, and listen to their gentle breathing and tried not to hear every move and every breath Yvette took.

SAM WAKENED the next morning to the sound of Gil and Tad whispering. They were by the stove. He cracked open his eyes, hoping everything had been a nightmare. Though last evening with Yvette would have been a sweet dream.

But he was still in the solid little cabin. Dawn still poked its way through narrow windows.

Yvette lay curled on her side, her hands folded at her face. Her lashes fanned on cheeks that captured the pink dawn. He didn't know how long he might have watched her, admiring her, if she hadn't opened her eyes and met his gaze. She didn't move. Didn't blink. Nor did he. The moment went on and on, measured in heartbeats that promised more.

She sighed, sat up, and looked around. "You're all still here." She sighed again. "I guess no one has found a way out."

Sam rose, pulled Yvette to her feet and they joined the boys at the stove. "There is one way out."

Three pairs of eyes jerked toward him.

"Fire." He knew it posed a great risk but it also provided hope.

Three mouths pressed into a line. Three heads rocked back and forth.

"I'm not keen to burn to death," Yvette said.

No one was ready to consider the idea. Maybe they never would be. He went to the cupboard and began a thorough investigation. They had water. Limited food but plenty enough for a week. But how long could they survive if Blackie didn't return? But there was no reason the man wouldn't return. Apart from accidents or …He turned his back to the cupboard. "Blackie will be a few days yet." Sam couldn't imagine anyone would pay him for Yvette if he didn't produce her. That meant he would need to take her to the fort. But what would he do with Sam? Or the boys, for that matter? Or would he simply give up on the idea as being too much work and ride away. And yet, they had little option but to hope and pray and wait for Blackie. And keep themselves amused until he returned. "I can teach you to make griddle cakes," he said to the others. "First, Yvette, let's get the beans cooking." There was little to add to them except salt and molasses. Good enough.

Then he showed each of them how to prepare batter for the griddle cakes.

"Of course, they'd be better if we had milk and eggs. But I don't think we have room in here for a cow and chickens."

Yvette looked up from mixing the batter and gave him a look of such disbelief that he roared with laughter.

Gil got down on all fours and, mooing like a cow, made his way around the room.

Tad, not to be outdone, put his thumbs in his armpits, flapped his elbows, gave some dramatic squawks, and strutted after his brother.

Yvette laughed at their antics. Her gaze returned to Sam's and her laughter ended, but her eyes continued to brim with amusement and something else that reached into his heart, making him aware of the air between them. Full of possibility and hope.

A feeling he needed to hang on to. And not just in connection with her. He needed to cling to the future and not let being stuck in a prison discourage him.

He showed Yvette how to fry pancakes. She ruined the first one trying to turn it but they couldn't waste food and she pressed it almost flat and finished cooking it. Her skill increased with each pancake.

They sat on the floor in a circle with plates or bowls on their laps.

"I'll say grace," Sam said. As he bowed his head, he realized there was much to be thankful for, despite the circumstances. "God in heaven, thank you for food, for good people to share the day with, for a warm, dry place to shelter in, for the sun and the sky—"

"And birds," Tad whispered. "They're singing."

Indeed, nearby, birds whistled and warbled.

"And for happy birds outside the window," Sam said then murmured, "Amen." He opened his eyes and looked into Yvette's.

A smile lingered at the corners of her mouth.

"What are you thinking?" he asked.

"About the fact I share this place with good people. Two sweet boys..." She bestowed a tender smile on each of the boys and they grinned with pleasure. "And a good, kind man." The smile she gave Sam ran through him like a beam of summer sunshine.

His mouth grew so dry he reached for a cup of

water, swallowed roughly, then bent his attention to the pancakes. He'd even found a can with a bit of syrup in it and rationed some out to everyone. He ate a mouthful. "Not bad for what we had to work with."

Yvette grinned. "Are you saying I did good?"

"You did very good."

The boys nodded vigorously and murmured agreement.

"Why, thank you all. It was fun." Her smile faded. Her expression grew guarded. Perhaps even sad.

Sam touched the back of her hand. "What happened to your smile?"

She smiled, but it lacked the depth of a few minutes ago.

He waited until they finished eating and the boys took the dishes to be washed before he pulled Yvette to her feet and led her to the farthest window.

"What's troubling you?"

"It's nothing. At least nothing anyone can do anything about."

"I'd like to know. Maybe together we can solve whatever it is."

Slowly she faced him. Her gaze drilled into his.

He felt the ache behind her eyes and caught her by the shoulders. "Yvette, what is it?"

She scrubbed her lips together, looked past him and then back at him and spoke in a tortured whisper. "You don't know how many times I've wished and prayed for what I have here."

"You wanted to be kidnapped and held prisoner?" Shock made his words crisp.

She shook her head. "Not that part. But having a simple home, happy children, and a man who—"

A man who what? How did she see him? Did she see a cowboy who could barely read or write? Who didn't own a thing but the horse Maude and John had given him? Who had lied to his sister about writing letters to her?

Dare he hope she saw a man who was willing to do anything to make others happy? Who especially wanted to make *her* happy? And who, in the dark night hours, had vowed he would sacrifice his own life for them if it meant they could go free?

She leaned forward, her gaze boring into his. "A man I could count on through good and bad. A man who cares deeply. Who lov—"

She didn't finish and he didn't press her to. He was certain she'd been about to say a man who loves.

The word pried open a door in his heart. Love. Was it possible for him? Oh, he knew Maude and John loved him. The other boys loved him in their own way. Even his horse loved him. That wasn't the sort of love he meant.

He hadn't forgotten how his parents had been around each other. The little glances across the table. The way Mama smiled when Pa touched her hand in passing. The lingering hug before Pa left for work.

That was the kind of love he ached for.

She lowered her gaze, making it impossible to guess at her thoughts.

Had she really imagined a life shared with him? Or was it simply desperation at being held prisoner that made her talk like that?

Yvette stared at a log in the wall. She hadn't meant to make Sam uncomfortable. She couldn't even explain why she'd said what she did. Except it rang with truth. She longed for a simple life where what she did mattered to the survival and well-being of those she loved and who loved her back. She might be imprisoned with no assurance as to how this would turn out, but she'd never regret the chance to get to know Sam better and learn to care for two little boys.

If—when—she got out, she would make sure those boys got a good home. With her.

And a husband?

She thought of the newspaper ad and her plans to write to an unknown man with a view to matrimony. What if he didn't like the boys? Well, she'd never marry someone who didn't accept them.

There was one man who wanted what was best for them.

Sam.

She smiled at the idea of Sam being a father. If

what she'd seen in this horrible situation meant anything, he'd be a great father. And a good husband.

Gil and Tad had washed the dishes and moved to stand before the adults.

"What is it?" Sam asked them.

"You know any more games?" Tad rocked back and forth in eagerness.

Sam tapped his finger to his mouth...a gesture that made Yvette study his face as never before. He had a strong jaw, full lips that begged to be kisse—

Whoa! How had she gone from thinking he was wrong to deceive his sister to this?

Except she no longer blamed him for letting Grace believe he'd written those letters. She understood his only motivation was to make life easier for her. Just as teaching her to cook and playing with the boys was to make their imprisonment less horrible.

"A game? You'd like a game?"

Both boys nodded.

Sam moved with such swiftness it stole Yvette's breath. One arm encircled each boy before any of them could think to move and he lifted them.

They screamed with laughter as he hopped across the room, shaking them with every step.

He pivoted and returned to Yvette's side as she watched them, smiling at their glee. He deposited them in front of her.

"More. More." Tad pulled on Sam's hand.

Again, with a speed that startled and awed Yvette,

he swept up both boys, tucked them under his arms, and shook them as he walked across the room.

They giggled so hard that it made Yvette laugh with them.

Sam circled and stopped in front of her, the boys still squirming and giggling in his arms. His gaze found hers and stopped. Neither of them moved or blinked. She wasn't even sure she breathed. Time froze on this moment when she saw him with her heart—a man to be trusted, who cared about others and was worthy of—

She didn't allow herself to finish the thought.

Gil escaped Sam's arm. He pulled Tad free and they tackled Sam. Sam pretended to be overpowered and fell to the floor. The boys bounced on his stomach and tickled him until Sam called, "Yvette, help. Help!"

She wasn't sure how she was supposed to help but didn't intend to miss this chance to play. She knelt beside Sam and joined the boys in tickling him.

He caught her hands and stilled them. "No fair. Three against one."

The boys stopped, perhaps wondering if they'd gone too far and he'd get angry. Indeed, he scowled at them all in a fearsome way.

But his hold on Yvette's hands was gentle, and she knew in the depths of her heart that he would never hurt any of them or respond in anger. She didn't know how she knew. She just did.

He gave a mighty roar, grabbed the two boys in one

hand and lurched to his feet, still holding Yvette in the other hand. He roared again and shook the boys. Then, before anyone could be frightened, he laughed. "Scared you, didn't I?"

The boys laughed. Yvette laughed too. But she didn't try and escape his hold.

Sam turned and smiled at her. "Did I scare you?"

Her eyes brimming with an emotion she couldn't even name, she shook her head. "You would never hurt anyone."

"Not anyone I cared about."

His words gave her the courage to believe he would protect her and the boys should the need arise.

The next hour was filled with laughter and roughhousing until Sam and the boys sank to the cot to rest.

Yvette sat on the chair, content to watch their play.

Silence filled the room.

A silence that was shattered by the sound of an approaching horse. Or was it a wild animal? Maybe the bear had returned to scratch at the window. How many hours…days would it take for the opening to be large enough for someone to crawl through?

Tad was the smallest, but she didn't like the idea of him going alone to face whatever was out there unless they made sure the bear was truly gone before he left. But how could they be certain?

The four of them rushed to peer out the narrow windows.

She couldn't see anyone. Or anything.

But the sound of horse steps was unmistakable.

Had rescue come or did it signal more danger? The sound faded. The four of them waited, listening. Had the rider left? Several minutes later, the clop of horses grew closer.

"I think it's Uncle." Gil's voice carried regret and resignation.

Yvette put her hand on his shoulder. When Sam put his on Tad's she looked at him. Met his gaze. Was this rescue? Or more trouble?

He folded his hand over her free one. "We are in this together."

His words chased away her fears. Or at least forced them into a small corner of her heart.

All eyes turned toward the door as the rasp of the bar informed them someone sought entry. The door swung open, half blinding Yvette with the brightness. She made out the shape of a man but couldn't see his face. Her heart took wings. Had someone come to free them?

"Decided ya need to come with me."

She recognized Blackie's voice. Her eyes adjusted and she saw the man clearly. Her wings were instantly clipped, letting her hopes crash.

"Gather up yer things and less be on our way."

No one moved. For her part, Yvette didn't know who he meant. All of them? Some of them?

Another possibility thundered through her head.

Perhaps only her?

She shifted to Sam's side. He put a steadying arm around her and she shamelessly, desperately pressed to him.

"Missy. I mean ya."

She didn't move. Couldn't move.

"We got beans cooked, Uncle," Gil said, hurrying to the stove and holding a spoon toward his uncle.

"I might as well eat." Blackie crossed the floor, took the spoon and ate right from the pot.

Sam pressed his mouth to Yvette's ear and whispered softly, "We'll all go. It's our only hope of escape."

She nodded. It was a good plan, but how were they to make Blackie agree?

Blackie finished, let out a loud belch and dropped the spoon on the floor.

Gil retrieved it, wiped it on a cloth and handed it to Tad. He filled bowls for Sam and Yvette then, taking turns, he and Tad ate hurriedly from the pot. As if fearing their uncle would notice and forbid it.

Blackie jabbed his finger toward Yvette. "Less go."

Sam's arm tightened around Yvette. "We're all going."

She wondered at his boldness. Wondered even more when Blackie pulled out his gun and aimed it at Sam's head.

"Who says?"

"I do," Sam said with deadly calm.

"Ha. Ha. Youse funny."

Ice frosted Yvette's veins at the glee in Blackie's eyes.

"Now le's go." He nodded at Yvette.

"We all go," Sam spoke with the same calm. The weight of his arm on her shoulders made it clear he didn't intend to release her.

"I don't mind shootin' ya." The click of his gun sent shivers through her.

She broke free of Sam's grasp and stood in front of him. "You'll have to shoot me too."

Blackie swore. "Yer aggravatin' me." He turned to the boys. "Tell 'em they don't want to aggravate me."

Neither boy moved nor spoke. But their wide eyes informed Yvette they didn't care to anger their uncle.

If—when—she got out of this, she would give those boys a kind and loving home. One where they felt safe.

Sam pulled Yvette behind him.

"Less go." Blackie waved toward the door, his gun still leveled on Sam. He backed from the room and waited just outside the door.

Sam held Yvette's hand and edged them forward. He caught up her valises as they passed the bed. Just before they stepped into the open, he stopped. "The boys are coming too. Gil, Tad, come on."

Yvette glanced over her shoulder. At first, the boys didn't move, then Gil took Tad's hand and they came to Yvette's side. She put an arm around each of them and held them close.

Blackie swore again. "Who died and made ya

boss?"

"I'm not going without all of them. You can shoot me or take us." Sam spoke boldly, fearlessly.

But Yvette expected any minute to hear Blackie's gun go off and Sam to fall to the floor.

"Shooting suits me jest fine."

Yvette would have pushed past Sam and put herself in front of him again, but he guessed at her thoughts and gripped the door frame on either side so that she couldn't get by. All she could do was press her forehead to his back and pray, murmuring the words aloud. "God save us all. Rescue us. Set us free."

"What's that?" Blackie bellowed.

"She's praying." Sam's voice carried the tiniest hint of humor. "Asking God to defend us."

Blackie swore again.

"You might not want to offend God," Sam said with conviction.

"I ain't got enough hosses for all of yas."

"The boys weigh almost nothing. I see you've got two horses and a packhorse ready to go. You and Yvette could each take a boy. I could ride on the packhorse."

Something about that amused Blackie and he chortled. "Kinda like to see ya on ole Packie, here. 'Ceptin' the missy will ride with me. Now less go."

Yvette swallowed hard. Blinked back fear.

Was being out of this cabin worth riding with Blackie?

7

Sam had no intention of making...or letting... Yvette ride with Blackie. The very idea made him curl his fists and think very unchristian-like thoughts of doing something hurtful to the man.

"Stay with me," he told the boys. He took Yvette by the hand, crossed to the horse nearest him and lifted her into the saddle, all the while ignoring Blackie's barked orders to put her on his horse.

He picked up Tad and put him in front of Yvette then lifted Gil to sit behind her on the horse's rump. The three of them together wouldn't weigh any more than either man. Then he climbed aboard the packhorse. Thankfully, Blackie only used side bags and not one of those cumbersome pack saddles. He positioned himself as best he could. It wasn't a natural way to ride, but he could do it.

Blackie muttered under his breath, looked at them

all with unveiled disgust, then swung to the back of his horse. He grabbed the reins of Yvette's horse. "Y'all best not be tryin' to get away. As to ya—" he gave Sam a dark look "—Ya can ride inta the woods for all I care." With that, he rode away.

Sam immediately followed Yvette's horse. He would not be riding away and leaving Yvette and the boys to deal with Blackie on their own.

Blackie rode down the narrow trail that had brought them here a few days ago. Sam could see enough of the sun to know they rode southeast. Toward Fort Macleod, he assumed. From what he'd observed on the ride to this place, he judged it to be at least three days ride from the fort. That would mean spending nights in the outdoors.

He shifted and tried to assess what the side bags held. But they were securely tied and he couldn't tell. Thankfully, Maude had made sure the boys knew how to survive in the open with limited supplies. He didn't think Blackie would care about the comfort of his companions, but Sam would be able to take care of Yvette and the boys as they traveled.

They rode with the sun in their faces, leaving the shelter of the trees and navigating a rugged, rocky strip of land that allowed him a view of the rolling hills. The breeze that rippled the golden grass carried the scent of pine. Trees dotted the hollows. Sunlight shimmered off the creek below them. But there were no buildings or cowboys in sight.

The sun climbed overhead then slanted rays across their shoulders. Recalling the previous trip, he guessed Blackie didn't consider a noon break necessary.

Sam rode closer to Yvette when the trail widened enough to make it possible. Yvette's horse was nose to rump with Blackie's horse, but the man didn't turn to check on the others. In fact, he'd only turned once, when they left the trees. Whether it was because he had to pick his way through the rocks or whether he simply didn't care how the others were doing, Sam was grateful that it allowed him to speak to Yvette and the boys.

"Everyone all right?" The breeze spoke louder than he did.

Yvette nodded, but her eyes revealed her worry and fear.

If only he could assure her they would be safe. He couldn't, but he would do his very best to protect all of them.

"We're playing *I Spy*," Tad said.

"That's nice." He shifted his attention to Gil, saw worry and fear in his eyes too.

He leaned over to squeeze Gil's arm. Then the trail narrowed and he fell back again.

As he had from the time they left the cabin, he studied his surroundings carefully. Perhaps he could see a chance to escape and a place to hide. Or someone to call to for help.

Their shadows lengthened and bounced across the

rocks. Still, they rode. Did Blackie never get weary? Or was he hoping to exhaust the others so they wouldn't have the strength or energy to try and escape?

Yvette slumped forward. Gil patted her back and she straightened.

If they didn't stop soon, it would be too dark to make a proper camp. But Sam knew if he said anything, it might well give Blackie delight to make them go on, so he held his peace.

But not since they'd left their dark prison had he stopped praying for God to rescue them. Not that he was opposed to helping God if a chance arose.

Blackie led them down an incline into a grove of trees and stopped. The flash of blue through the leaves of the bushes revealed he'd chosen a spot with water.

Ashes in a circle of stones informed Sam this had been a previously used camping spot.

Blackie dismounted. "We's spendin' the night here." He made no effort to help Yvette or the boys and Sam jumped down to do so. But Blackie stopped him.

"Theys can take care of their selves." He held out a length of rope. "Hands behind ya."

Sam crossed his arms over his chest. "I don't think so."

Blackie snorted. He grabbed Gil, yanked him to the ground and whipped the rope across the boy's back. "This is what happens if ya think ya have a choice."

Sam's knuckles popped as he squeezed his fists. The man might have a gun and a rope, but Sam was not about to let him bully the boys. He took a step forward.

Blackie grabbed Yvette and dragged her from the horse. She landed in a heap. She bit her lip to keep from crying out, but Sam saw the pain in her eyes.

Blackie raised a boot.

Sam saw red as he realized Blackie meant to kick her.

"No!" He leaped forward.

Blackie swung his hand.

Sam realized he held his pistol and he meant to use it, but before he could react, Blackie laid a blow with the butt of the gun on Sam's head. Stars flashed before his eyes. The world tipped. His face met the ground. He tasted dirt. Felt grass between his teeth. Then nothing.

He opened his eyes. Tried to touch the painful area on his temple but couldn't move. Mentally, he explored his body. His hands were behind him. Couldn't bring them forward. Tied. He was tied. His feet were also tied. He tried to move and realized he was bound to a tree.

He blinked to clear his vision. It was dark. Coals of a campfire glowed several feet away. Squinting to focus his eyes, he looked for clues as to where they were, where the others were.

"Yvette." The whispered word sounded like thunder in his head.

"I'm here." He turned to the sound of her voice at his right. "Are you all right?"

"Yeah, I think so."

"You were out a long time."

"Where are the boys?"

"Beside me. Tied up so they can't move. I think they're asleep. Poor little fellas are exhausted."

"And Blackie?" Part of him hoped the man had left them. A more reasonable part said they needed him to untie them or someone might find their bones next to the trees.

"He's across the fire. Hear him snoring?"

Sam listened. "Guess I do."

"You've got to stop letting him hit you on the head."

Sam gave one chuckle then stopped, deciding he would save his amusement for another day. "Did he feed you? Treat you well?"

"He was a perfect gentleman."

Her droll tone made him grimace. "Don't make me laugh. It hurts my head."

"Sorry."

"I am too. I couldn't help you." He should have been more careful so he could be awake for the evening. "Are the boys all right? He didn't whip them any more did he?"

"No. He made them take care of the fire, but as soon as we ate, he tied us all up."

"He fed you?" He wouldn't have been surprised if Blackie didn't bother.

"Biscuits and jerky. Water."

"Do I smell coffee? Or am I dreaming?"

Yvette's chuckle seemed sadly lacking in humor. "He made a pot full but never offered me any. Doubt if he'll offer us any come morning, either."

"The first thing I'm getting when we reach the fort is a decent cup of that stuff."

"The first thing I'm going to do is have a bath." She paused. "And then I'll join you for coffee."

Was it his aching head that made him hear eagerness for that occasion?

Well, of course, she was as anxious to be free as he was.

She spoke again. "Do you have any sense of where we are?"

"Vaguely. We are south of Circle A Ranch. On our way to Fort Macleod."

"How long before we reach the fort?"

He didn't want to tell her all the variables. "The most direct route would get us there day after tomorrow."

She made a considering sound. "What is it you aren't telling me?"

What was the point in revealing his worries?

"Sam, don't treat me like I need to be handled with kid gloves. I can deal with the truth."

He thought of the rolling hills with little in the way

of hiding places. Would Blackie choose to ride in the open where any passing cowboy could spot them? Curious and friendly, and perhaps a tiny bit lonely, the rider would likely gallop up to say howdy.

No, he didn't think Blackie would want that.

Wouldn't he rather stick to the rocky embankments where he would be less visible?

He explained his reasoning to Yvette.

"I believe you're right. Are you saying it might take us more than a day and a half to get there?"

"That would be my guess." Keep south. Stay in the mountains. Perhaps not even go to the fort. Blackie might insist whoever brought ransom money had to accompany him to a hiding place away from the fort where the Mounties lived.

"At least he hasn't tied us up while we're riding."

Sam didn't say anything. But he wondered how long before Blackie realized Sam could ride for help.

"Go to sleep," he said. "I expect we'll have a long day tomorrow."

"You sleep too. Good night."

"Good night," he murmured. But there was something more he needed to say. "Yvette?"

"I'm awake. What is it?"

"I'm sorry I haven't been able to get us out of this mess. But I promise you, I won't leave you on your own to deal with that man."

"Sam, first of all, this mess, as you call it, is not your fault. It's because of my father's money. And secondly, if you get a chance to ride away, please take it. It might be our only hope of rescue."

"Umm." Let her think that meant whatever she wanted it to.

"Sam, promise. Besides, I don't think I can survive seeing you knocked out again. Twice is twice too many."

He heard the shudder in her voice. The words came out unevenly as if she struggled to say them. He smiled, ignoring how the movement made his head hurt. It sounded like she cared beyond simple human kindness. Of course, he understood it was due to their situation. If—when—she was safely reunited with her family, she would remember that Sam was only a cowboy. But for now, he would enjoy being more.

"Sam?" she prompted. "Promise."

"Yvette, I promise this. I will not leave you and the boys unless you are safe, free of Blackie."

Her breath whooshed out. "That's not what I asked." Her voice deepened. "But it's what I expected. Thank you."

Several feet of distance separated them and yet her words were like a physical touch. One of blessing, healing, and delight. If his hands were free and he was able to move, he would have hugged her. Held her in his arms until she fell asleep. Then he would stay there throughout the night, dozing, if he slept at all, as he guarded her until morning.

He would fight Blackie and anyone or anything that threatened her safety and happiness.

If only Blackie wasn't so quick to smash Sam's head.

Sam might want to defy the man, but he couldn't protect Yvette and the boys if he died at the side of the trail. Or even if he lay unconscious while they rode on.

YVETTE CLOSED HER EYES, a smile on her face. Sam would defend her and the boys. Even if it cost him. It was a comforting thought. But also a frightening one. She was quite certain that Blackie would not hesitate to shoot Sam and leave him.

Lord, seems I am always calling on You to help me. But without You, we are pawns in Blackie's plans. Please keep us safe. Especially keep Sam safe.

Dawn kissed the eastern horizon when Blackie hollered at them all to wake up. He freed the boys.

"Get some wood. Fill the pot with water."

The boys scrambled to obey.

Blackie approached Sam who watched him warily. "See yer alive. Too bad." Blackie lifted his boot and kicked Sam's shoulder.

Yvette bit her lip to keep from crying out.

Sam flinched but gave no other response.

"Yer no use ta me. Got a good mind to leave ya here."

The look Sam gave Blackie should have burned the skin clean off the man, but he only cackled as if he got pleasure out of tormenting him.

"Guess I'll take ya along fer the pleasure of seeing ya suffer."

Sam glowered at the man.

Blackie turned his attention to Yvette. "This here is all that matters." He untied her hands.

She pulled them forward and rubbed them.

"Gotta get ya back in one piece." He looked thoughtful. "Or at least make 'em think so." He looked at Gil squatted by the fire, tending a pot of mush. "Less eat and get goin'"

Yvette struggled to her feet, balancing on her bound feet, then hopped into the bushes to take care of her personal needs.

"Need any help?" Blackie chortled.

She didn't respond. Nor did she hurry. She struggled to loosen the ropes around her ankles. There had to be something she could do to escape this man. Run into the woods? Hide from him in bushes? He'd come after her, but he'd have to catch her. He'd have to leave Sam and the boys to follow her. Would they be able to get away before he caught her?

"Ain't gonna let ya go."

She startled at Blackie's voice so close. He stood in the shadows with a feral grin on his face.

"Couldn't loosen the rope, could ya?"

She might have been able to do so given a little more time. But the opportunity was past.

He grabbed her arm, his fingers digging into her flesh, and hustled her back to the camp. She could barely hop fast enough to keep up. He shoved her to the ground.

"Eat if'n you want. We leaves soon."

Gil handed her a tin cup with mush. Nothing more.

She ate it, her gaze darting to Blackie as he leaned back enjoying a cup of coffee. "What about Sam?" she asked.

"He's lucky to be alive."

"He hasn't had anything to eat or drink since yesterday morning."

Blackie shrugged.

She got to her feet. "I'll feed him." She hobbled over without waiting for Blackie to say yay or nay. She tensed with each hop, expecting to be dragged back, but Blackie seemed intent on enjoying his coffee.

She knelt in front of Sam and offered him a spoonful of the mush.

"Thirsty," he croaked.

Gil trotted over with a cup of water, ignoring his uncle's muttered complaint that they didn't need to think he wasn't watching.

Tad followed his brother.

Gil held the cup to Sam's lips and Sam drank the entire contents.

"Thanks." He studied Gil and then Tad. "You two all right?"

Both boys nodded then darted a look at Blackie.

Tad leaned closer to whisper, "Uncle hurt you."

"I'm fine," Sam assured him. "Remember, we are in this together and God is with us."

Yvette fed him the mush. She'd barely finished when Blackie sprang to life.

"'Nough of that. Less get goin'. Gil, pack up the things. Tad, douse the fire."

Gil took the cups, quickly swished them with water and packed the bags that had been on the packhorse.

Tad ran to the creek to get water to pour on the fire.

Yvette remained where she was, hoping for…

What? That he would leave them? If only he would. She'd untie her feet and free Sam. They would walk someplace and get help.

But of course, that wasn't to be.

Blackie pulled a horse close to Yvette and untied her feet. She hurried to mount the horse before he could touch her, but she couldn't make it on her own. Chortling, Blackie pushed on her bottom.

"Might be I'll stop earlier tonight and have me some fun."

She settled herself in the saddle, swallowing back rising bile at what he meant.

Gil and Tad hovered nearby.

Fear clawed through her insides as Blackie squinted at his nephews and then Sam. Would he leave the others behind? Or would he take the boys and leave Sam, tied and helpless?

She left her feet out of the stirrups. If Blackie thought to take her and leave any of the others, he would have a fight on his hands. She'd jump from this horse and fight him with all her might. She would not give in to such plans. Ever.

Blackie growled low in his throat as he stared at Sam. "Jest as soon leave ya here."

Gil pushed Tad behind him as he faced his uncle. "Please don't do that, Uncle. He hasn't done anything wrong."

"'Cept make a nuisance of hisself." He kicked at Sam's feet.

"I'll untie him." Gil tackled the ropes at Sam's feet.

Yvette held her breath, expecting Blackie to protest and even strike the boy. Instead, he pulled the horses forward.

Tad tackled the ropes tying Sam to the tree. The boys struggled with the knots, but Blackie ignored them as he tightened cinches and checked the packs.

Finally, Sam shook off the ropes. "Be right back." He trotted into the trees.

Blackie snorted. "Lookee that. He's goin' skip out on ya."

"No, he won't," Tad insisted.

The boys watched where Sam had gone and grinned widely when he returned.

"We knew you wouldn't leave us," Tad said, sending an I-told-you-so glance in his uncle's direction.

Sam lifted the boys to sit in front of and behind Yvette.

He paused with his hand on her knee. "We will stick together until we reach safety."

She pressed her hand to his. "Sam." Her throat closed off and she couldn't say more. But her nod seemed to satisfy him as he climbed to the back of the packhorse.

Gil whispered in her ear. "I'm glad Sam is with us. He makes me feel safe."

"Me, too," she said, her words soft. She knew there was little he could do without incurring Blackie's wrath and yet it was comforting, encouraging, to know he was there. Prepared to do his best.

Blackie grunted. Seemed to consider the situation. Then tied Sam's hands. He reached under the horse as if to tie his feet then appeared to think better of it. Instead, he tied a lead rope to the animal Yvette rode, mounted his horse and they were on their way.

As Sam had suspected, they stayed along the ridge among the rocks and trees. The view to her left was awe-inspiring. It reminded her of a verse in Psalms. She said it aloud for the boys to hear and maybe even Sam.

Whether or not Blackie heard was immaterial to her.

"The Bible says, 'The earth is the Lord's, and the fulness thereof; the world, and they that dwell therein. For He hath founded it upon the seas, and established it upon the floods.' It's good for us to remember He is with us. He will take care of us."

"Can Mama and Papa see us?" Tad asked.

She considered her answer carefully. "I guess I don't know. But maybe God or an angel tells them how you're doing."

Neither boy responded.

Oh, how her heart ached to think of this pair having only someone like Blackie to care for them. But not much longer. When she got to safety, the boys were staying with her.

To amuse them, she told stories and played little games with them. She spoke softly so as to not draw Blackie's attention.

Often she glanced back at Sam. He followed as close as he could but the trail was too narrow for him to ride beside her. Most times he watched her and his eyes spoke courage and strength to her. So long as he was with her, she knew everything would be all right.

Blackie drew to a stop and muttered an oath. He looked toward the valley.

She followed the direction of his gaze. In the distance, two dots moved. Riders. So far away they were like ants.

She waved, hoping they would see.

They had been riding with a cliff to their right, the river to their left and beyond that, the rolling hills. Blackie turned to the right and urged his horse upward. The horses struggled to climb the bank.

Gil clung to her. She clamped her arms around Tad and prayed they wouldn't fall. Or be crushed if the horse lost its footing.

They reached the top. It was a narrow bit of land with trees crowding to the right. She expected Blackie to head into the woods, where no one could see him. Instead, he kept on the trail that was barely wide enough for a horse.

Her horse's hoof slipped. Her heart clawed up her throat. She was about to go over the edge to the rushing waters below, taking two little boys with her.

"Careful," Sam murmured. "Take your time."

She was doing the best she could, but his words steadied her. She tried to relax and let the horse pick its way along the treacherous path.

Ahead of her, Blackie muttered and complained.

She stared as he suddenly went lower. Did the trail drop?

The ground trembled beneath them. It sighed and then roared.

The ground disappeared. They were hurtling through space. Rocks and dirt rumbled alongside them.

Gil hung on so tight she could hardly breathe.

Though her lungs had refused to work. She wrapped her arms around Tad.

"God save us," she hollered.

Her feet slipped from the stirrups. The horse screamed as it fell.

They tumbled after it.

8

Sam knew when the dirt had slipped away under the hoof of Yvette's horse that the bank was unstable. But still, the suddenness with which it gave way made him gasp.

His heart hammered at a frantic pace to see Yvette, her horse, and the boys tumbling from the disappearing trail. "Yvette," he hollered, but he doubted anyone heard him above the roar of falling earth. Besides, what did he expect they would do? Change their minds about going over the edge?

Knowing his horse might follow them, he began to urge him to back up. One step and the ground gave way. He was falling. Below him lay the rushing water, bushes, trees, and scattered boulders that would dash a man's bones to powder. Yvette's horse hit the water with a splash. He couldn't see Yvette or the boys. His mind moved in slow motion as he tried to think of what to do.

His horse went one way. He went another which was fine with him. He did not want to have the animal fall on him or with him. His hands were tied, leaving him helpless to break his fall. Seems his head was hard enough to endure blows. Maybe he could land on it.

He hit the water. And sank to the bottom. Kicking his feet and flapping his arms, he made it to the surface and gasped for air.

Where were the others? Had they landed in the water? Or on rocks?

He paddled as best he could with bound hands, looking around for something to hold on to. A log floated nearby and he splashed toward it. Downstream, he made out two horses and two heads but couldn't see who it was. He must free his hands if he was to help anyone.

Using his teeth he loosened ropes he'd been working on since they left camp. Thankfully, he'd almost succeeded in undoing the first knot and he finished it in record time taking no heed for how the rope bruised and tore at his lip.

Frantic at the speed with which the others were carried downstream, he freed himself and swam toward them.

Gil and Tad clung to overhanging branches. Safe for now. Until their hands grew weak. Or a drifting log dislodged them. He was torn between getting them to safety or leaving them so he could locate Yvette.

"Stay there," he called. "I'll come for you as soon as I find Yvette." He swam on, his heart pounding out a constant prayer. *God, save her. Save us all by Your mighty hand.*

The side bags were caught in the bushes at the bank. Blackie's hat hung from a limb.

Sam swam past them. He shook his head to clear the water from his eyes. Ahead he caught a glimpse of gray fabric. Was it Yvette's skirt? He swam closer. She clung to a boulder, the current pressing her to it.

"Yvette!" The word ached from him.

She turned at his call. Her eyes were wide and bottomless. Her pupils were so large only a rim of the irises remained.

He was soon at her side. "Are you all right? Can you move?"

"The boys," she gasped.

"They're safe. Come on, I'll get you to the bank, and then we'll go to them." He held her as he swam the few yards to the edge of the river. A foot or two of gravel gave them a place to stand.

He helped her to solid ground then held her to his chest. "I thought…" He couldn't give words to all the flashing pictures that had raced through his mind. "Never mind." He caught her upper arms and eased her back so he could see her face better. "You're safe. That's all that matters."

With a shudder that shook her from head to toe, she leaned into his embrace, her arms encircling his waist. "Thank God you're alive."

"Amen. Now let's get the boys out of the water." But he couldn't make himself let go of her. He closed his eyes. She was safe, but his heart might never recover from the thought of losing her. He'd grown unreasonably fond of the spoiled rich girl. In fact, he might be wrong in his assessment. She was spunky and...

It was Yvette straightening and taking his hand, holding it with a grip that surprised and pleased him with its strength, that enabled him to hurry back to where he'd seen the boys. His heart released a joyful beat to see they were still there.

"Stay here," he told her as he slipped into the water. He took Tad first and handed him up to Yvette.

She crushed the boy to her then watched, her expression anxious, as he returned for Gil. "Hurry, he's slipping away."

The bush Gil clung to ripped from the ground and swept away with Gil still holding on.

The current seemed to have grown stronger and Gil was carried downstream.

"Sam," Gil's damp, desperate voice reached Sam and then the bush twisted and Gil was lost from sight.

"Sam!" Yvette whispered. "He's gone." She pressed Tad to her side.

"I'll get him." Knowing that his boots could hinder

him, Sam took the time to pry them from his feet and then dived into the water.

He swam after the boy and the bush. The current was fast and it took several minutes before he gained on the floating debris. And several more before he reached the bush. He grabbed the branches and reached for Gil. But he wasn't there. Had he fallen off?

"Gil! Gil," he roared.

"Sam!" A head popped out from under a leafy tangle.

"Thank God you're safe. Now let's get you to dry land." He freed the boy from the bush, all the while clinging to him lest he be carried away. "Now hang on." With Gil under one arm, kicking to stay afloat, they swam across the current and finally made it to safety.

Sam dragged himself and Gil to the gravel verge. He ran his hands up and down Gil's side. "Are you hurt? Anything broken?"

"I don't think so."

Sam knew shock and cold would disguise a lot of injuries but all four of the boy's limbs worked. That was good enough for now. "You gave me quite a scare."

"Falling into the river was scary." The words sobbed from Gil.

He wrapped an arm around Gil and held him tight. "It certainly was. Can't say I ever want to do that again." He gave the boy a moment to compose himself.

"Let's go find the others and then figure out what we're going to do."

Gil didn't move. "What about Uncle?"

"I haven't seen him. Maybe he's further downstream."

"I hope he drowned."

Sam wasn't about to argue that matter.

"Is it bad for me to say that?"

"I don't think so. He hasn't been nice to you." He didn't add that the man didn't deserve to live. As Maude said about a scoundrel who had bothered them a few years ago, he was a waste of a perfectly good body.

Sam got to his feet and pulled Gil up. They headed upstream, their progress slowed by the gravel jabbing into Sam's stockinged feet.

He stopped. "I think this is where I saw the side packs. You stay here. I'm going to see if they're still there." He stepped into the water, clinging to the bushes as he edged around, looking for the packs. One thing about it. He couldn't get any wetter. And although he was cold, he knew he would get colder if they didn't find a dry place before nightfall.

The packs were still there and he carried them to Gil's side. Water rushed from them.

"Don't guess there'll be anything that isn't soaking wet," Gil said, his tone so morose that Sam chuckled.

"Some things will dry." Like the blankets. But most foodstuff would be ruined. He shook the packs to remove as much water as possible then continued back to where he'd left Yvette and Tad.

"Gil. Sam. You're all right."

Sam looked up from picking his way across the gravel. Yvette and Tad ran toward them, his boots carried by Yvette.

"Everyone is safe," he said as they hugged each other.

"Except Blackie," she whispered.

"I don't aim to go looking for him," he murmured close to her ear.

"He won't give up easily." She leaned back. "I'm worth money to him."

It was on the tip of his tongue to say she was worth more than money to *him*. But his heart swelled like it couldn't contain the thought and words were impossible.

They needed someplace to dry out. He looked around. A bank similar to the one that had caved in under them rose to the side. Above that were trees and sunshine. "Can we make it up there?"

"Sure can." Gil and Tad began to scramble up the embankment.

Sam struggled to pull on his wet boots but his feet were too tender to go without them.

Yvette waited at his side. As soon as he straightened, she caught his hand. He looked into her worried face.

"We'll be all right," he said, touching her cheek.

"How? We're wet and cold with no food or shelter."

He smiled, pleased he could offer her an answer. "Maude insisted we all learn basic survival skills. She said you could never be sure you wouldn't get stranded somewhere without anything but your wits. We'll manage. Trust me."

She caught his hands and squeezed. "I trust you."

Did she realize what a gift she'd given him? From considering him a poor specimen of a human for tricking Grace to now trusting him to take care of her and the boys? It made him feel like he could do anything. And he *would* do anything, everything to protect them and get them to safety. He scanned the rushing waters. There was no sign of Blackie or any of the horses. But that didn't mean the man wasn't this very minute stomping toward them. But maybe he'd lost his gun. Without it, Sam would not hesitate to fight the man. He could easily overpower him.

He grabbed the heavy packs. "Let's catch up to the boys." He let Yvette go first. Several times he placed a hand on her back to stop her from skidding on the loose shale.

They reached the top where the boys waited.

Sam paused to catch his breath, then led the way into the trees. "This is what we need." A small clearing facing south, allowing the sunlight to warm it. He dropped the packs to the ground. He struggled with the wet ropes but managed to open them. More water drained out as he folded back the canvas. He removed the contents. Tin dishes which would come in handy if they had food. *When* they had food, he reminded himself.

Four blankets. He wrung the water from them then hung them over a branch to dry. A knife with a six-inch blade. Sam could use that. His own pocketknife was too small to be useful for what he'd need, and the blade dulled from digging at the logs. He set the long knife beside the dishes. Next, he removed bullets. So even if Blackie still had the gun and it still worked, he didn't have much in the way of ammo. More and more this was looking good.

There was a black, oiled slicker and a rolled-up piece of canvas that Blackie likely used for protection against the elements.

Sam spread both out to dry.

He opened the second pack. This was where Blackie had kept the food. Sam removed a sack of beans. "We can use these." They'd have to be dried. "And these." He took out four cans of peaches and some beans. The cornmeal and flour were ruined. The beef jerky had been wrapped in oil cloth and would be usable. The matches were wet, but there was a flint. Perfect. They had everything they needed to survive.

He removed a heavy coat and hung it. Water ran from it.

A bundle lay at the bottom and Sam removed it. He folded back the oil cloth to reveal a wad of bills and some gold coins.

He sat back on his heels and stared up at Yvette. "He had all this money. Why did he want more?" Why would he kidnap Yvette to get it?

"Someone once asked my father how much money was enough. He said, 'A little more.' Guess Blackie believed the same thing."

Gil touched the money. "Was he rich?"

Sam thumbed through the bills. "Not rich. But he could have afforded a few things." Like a proper house for the boys to live in. He could even have paid someone to take care of them. Except he was too selfish. And too greedy. Sam glanced over his shoulder. How long before Blackie tracked them down?

Now was not the time to worry about it.

"Let's get a fire going and get everyone dried out."

"Without matches?" Yvette sounded as if Sam had overlooked the fact the matches were soaked.

"It can be done. Boys, we need some tinder. Something that ignites easily. Like birch bark. There's a birch tree here." He went to it and stripped off some bark. He showed the boys how to shred it. "Then we need kindling and dry wood." All four of them searched the nearby trees for twigs and branches.

Yvette dragged back a fallen tree.

Sam was able to break off pieces of it—branches and small sections. He arranged the kindling and wood, then bent over the tinder and, using the knife, struck the flint. A few minutes later, he had a fire going. The boys cheered and Yvette clapped. "You amaze me."

"It's nothing." Yet it felt like something to know he had an ability that impressed her. The four of them huddled around the fire, steam rising from them as the water evaporated from their clothes.

They turned back and forth, drying both sides. As they grew warmer, they grew more talkative.

Over and over, the boys repeated the details of the fall and their rescue. After each telling, they would look toward the river. From the worry in their faces, Sam knew they wondered when Blackie would show up. He wondered too and made sure to keep the big knife with him. His own pocketknife was not much of a weapon, but the bigger one was a different matter.

He sent the boys to find more wood. As soon as they were gone, he spoke to Yvette.

"I don't know what happened to Blackie, but for now we're on our own. I suggest we spend the night here and get dried out. Then we can follow the river downstream until we reach the fort." He thought it would take three days on foot, though not knowing exactly where they were made it difficult for him to estimate.

Never mind. He'd do whatever it took to get them to safety.

"Whatever you think best. I trust you." She spoke with confidence; as if willing to place her life and her future in his hands. Not that she had a choice.

He smiled at her. It was a good feeling.

She shivered.

"You're cold. I'll make you something hot to drink." He hadn't poked through all the food supplies, but Blackie must carry coffee beans with him.

YVETTE HOVERED AS close to the fire as she dared. The side of her facing the flames was uncomfortably hot, but her insides were like winter. Her clothes were damp and icy. She couldn't stop shivering.

Thank you, God, that we're all safe. She excluded Blackie from her gratitude because she didn't want to ever see him again. *Thank you, too, that Sam is here and knows what to do.* It was comforting to know she was safe with him.

He returned with a pot of water and set it over the fire. While it heated he dug through the stuff from the packs.

"Yes! I knew there had to be coffee beans."

She chuckled at his enthusiasm. He ground some beans between two rocks, then dumped the grinds into the water.

It boiled. The aroma went a long way toward warming her insides.

He dipped out a cup of coffee and handed it to her.

She held it to her lips and inhaled the scent.

Sam watched and waited.

She met his eyes over the rim of the cup. His look spoke volumes of concern and caring for her. A rush of emotions blocked her throat. Thank goodness she didn't have her mouth full of coffee because she wouldn't have been able to swallow.

The boys returned, arms laden with wood.

Sam helped them then returned to Yvette. "Are you any warmer?"

She gulped a large mouthful of hot liquid and swallowed it loudly. Heat seared her throat and filled her stomach and dissipated as quickly as her next breath. "Maybe a little." But she couldn't stop shivering.

He touched her shoulder. A jolt raced to her heart and pooled there. A tiny bit of warmth in the midst of her cold body.

"How many layers do you have on under this?"

"A few," she admitted, too embarrassed by his question and her own silly thoughts to look directly at him.

"May I suggest you take off as many things as you can and hang them to dry? You'll warm up much faster."

"But—" She sputtered. She couldn't imagine removing anything without a private place. "What if Blackie comes back and sees me?"

"Let me look around. If there's no sign of him, you can hide behind the bushes. No one will spy on you." He trotted toward the river. A few minutes later he returned. "I didn't see him."

She nodded but didn't move.

He took her elbow and rubbed his hands up and down her arms, distracting her from her cold. But despite the warmth in her heart, she couldn't stop shivering.

"Yvette, I am worried about how cold you are and there's nothing dry to wrap you in." He guided her toward a thicket of bushes as he talked. "You need to get warm." He stopped and backed away. "Your shirt and skirt will dry more quickly if there aren't wet things under them. I'll wait at the fire. Don't be long." He touched her cheek, his fingers trailing toward her chin where they lingered.

Heat followed the path his fingers took. His touch made her feel—she wasn't sure she could find a word to describe how she felt—cherished?

And he was gone.

Her heart beat a question. Her brain stalled on her last thought. But her feet did not move. Then cold took over and with clumsy fingers, she struggled with buttons and ties. She managed to remove everything but her shift and drawers, then put her skirt and shirtwaist back on.

Between the cold and her fear that Blackie would suddenly materialize out of the shadows, her fingers were clumsy and her movements jerky. What if he was spying on her this very minute? He could snatch her and drag her away before Sam could stop him.

No. She'd call out. Sam would come to her rescue. She knew it without a shadow of a doubt.

Calmed, she hung her things over the bushes to dry.

"Yvette," Sam called. "Everything all right?"

She hurried back to the fire and held her hands out to the heat, avoiding looking directly at him for fear he would read her thoughts. "I kept thinking I heard someone or something in the woods." Remembering that Blackie was out there, she studied the trees surrounding them.

"We can defend ourselves from him if he shows up."

Yvette tried to think what Sam meant.

He touched the knife he'd taken from the packs.

She leaned closer so the boys wouldn't hear. "That's no defense against a gun."

"I'm hoping he lost his gun. Even if he didn't, I'm counting on him having limited shells." He told her of what he'd found in the packs.

Yvette took some comfort in that knowledge. But only for a moment. "He's not going to let me go."

"He's not going to get you back." Sam's voice cracked with hardness.

The warmth that seeped through her body had nothing to do with the fire she hovered over. And everything to do with his protectiveness.

She held her hands over the flames and reveled in the heat. To be warmed was nice, but to be valued was a true bit of wonderful.

Gil and Tad watched the adults. Their eyes were wide and often darted to the trees.

She looked at Sam. "They're worried."

"I know. I'll see what I can do to divert them." He reached for a can of peaches and the package of jerky. "Anyone hungry?"

Gil and Tad brought their gaze to him. "We are."

He divided the can of peaches and handed out a piece of jerky to each. "I'll say grace."

The boys watched Sam, their eyes full of trust.

Yvette smiled, knowing they felt as safe with Sam as she did. She bowed her head as he prayed.

"Thank you, God, for saving us from the waters. Thank you for being with us this very minute and promising to always be with us. Thank you for fire and food and water. Amen."

The boys began to eat but then Gil paused.

"Sam, are we going to die here?"

Sam set aside his empty bowl. "I can't promise you how long you will live. That's in God's hands, but we aren't going to die here. We'll eat, get dry and spend the night and then we'll walk out."

"Where will we go?" Tad's eyes were wide with worry.

"We'll follow the river until we reach the fort."

"How long?"

Yvette waited for the answer as desperately as the boys did.

"However long it takes. I am not going to stop

walking until we get there and I know you all feel the same way. Am I right?"

Gil and Tad looked at each other, then back to Sam. They nodded.

Three pairs of eyes turned toward Yvette. Did they think she was the weak one of the group? She sat up straight. "I can walk as far as I need to." Her voice rang with determination. Then she grinned. "After all, I've got three fine gentlemen to help me."

"I'll help you," Gil said.

"I'm just a boy," Tad sounded confused. "Not a gentleman."

"You're a fine boy. Remember how you sang to me? That's encouraging and I like that."

"Oh. All right." Tad beamed.

Sam edged closer to Yvette. "So now I'm a gentleman?"

Did she detect a hint of longing in his voice? "I regret the hurtful things I've said to you in the past. They were untrue. You are indeed a fine gentleman." She met his steady, hungry gaze. It pleased her to think her opinion mattered to him.

Hungry for more than food, she touched his hand. "Sam, you are my hero."

"Hero?" He gulped audibly. "You're forgetting I'm nothing but a poor cowboy."

A poor, lonely cowboy. The thought flashed in her mind like a bolt of lightning.

A lonely cowboy. A lonely rich girl. Two lonely hearts that found each other.

She shoved aside the errant thoughts. He waited as if wanting…needing… to hear her refute his statement. "I can't think of anyone I'd sooner be with at this moment than a cowboy with skills and a caring heart to guide us to safety." She pressed his hand again then lifted her palms to the heat of the fire. But the warmth in her heart came from having been able to bring a smile to Sam's face.

The simple meal was soon over. Sam held a blanket over the heat. "I need to get these dry before nightfall."

"I can help," Yvette said.

He gave her a blanket.

Seeing what they were doing, Gil and Tad insisted on helping as well. The four of them turned the blankets from side to side. The smell of damp wool and mildew rose with the steam. A breeze came up, chilling Yvette.

Sam moved, placing himself to block the wind from reaching her. "Are your clothes dry?" he asked.

"Getting there. I doubt I'm any damper than the rest of you." They were all destined for a clammy night.

"But we've endured hardships before."

"And you don't think I have?" She knew what he meant but intended to tease him.

"I doubt you've ever been stranded in the woods with nothing but wet clothes to wear."

"You're right. I haven't. How many times has it happened to you?"

He chuckled. "This is a first. But Maude taught us to be resourceful. On several occasions when we first arrived, she would send us out to survive on our own."

He must have heard her gasp and chuckled. "I'm pretty sure she wasn't too far away. Always checking on us. But it was for our own good. It taught us how to work together. And how to survive on our own." He chuckled again. "It was fun."

Gil and Tad sidled close. "Tell us about it."

So while they did their best to dry the blankets, Sam told them of times they spent in an old cabin or in a cave. The boys were fascinated with hearing about the cave.

"Can we see it sometime?" Gil asked.

"Don't see why not," Sam said. "I could take you there. And to the waterfalls. And to see the hoodoos."

"Hoodoos?" That sparked another burst of questions as the boys wanted to know all about that formation.

Yvette listened as keenly as the boys.

"Can Yvette come too?" Tad asked.

Sam looked at her. His eyes were shadowed so she couldn't make out what he was thinking.

"That would be up to Yvette."

She felt his waiting. And knew without knowing how what he needed her to say.

"Sam, I would love to see all those things with you."

She was rewarded by a quick smile. A sense of something she could only call peace settled over them.

Strange to think of peace under the circumstances, but except for the fear of Blackie finding them, she couldn't recall a time when she'd felt more settled in her heart.

"The sun is setting," Sam said.

She turned to watch the sky blaze pink and orange as the sun disappeared behind the mountains.

They watched until there was nothing but a blare of yellow at the horizon.

"We need to get some sleep," Sam said. He touched each blanket. "I think the blankets are reasonably dry. If we stay close to the fire we'll be warm enough."

The boys each took a blanket, but they didn't lie down.

Tad sidled close to Yvette. "Where are you sleeping?"

"Right there." She pointed to a spot near her feet.

"Me too."

She hugged him. "That's good. I'll feel much better if you're beside me."

Tad didn't move and Gil waited as if wanting to make sure his little brother was settled before he thought of sleep.

"Why don't you lie here and I'll sing for you." At Yvette's words, Tad nodded and settled on the ground. Gil lay at his side, one arm around his brother.

Yvette tucked the blankets around them and sang

softly. "'Savior, like a shepherd lead us, much we need Thy tender care. In Thy pleasant pastures feed us…'"

Tad closed his eyes and sighed.

The boys relaxed. Within minutes, their breathing deepened.

Yvette smoothed her hand over their backs and straightened. "Poor little guys are exhausted," she said. She covered a yawn.

"You must be tired."

The concern in his voice was as calming as if he'd rubbed her back like she'd done a few minutes ago to the boys. "I don't imagine I am any more tired than you."

"You get comfortable while I get some more wood." He disappeared into the trees.

She sat on the ground, the blanket around her, and stared at the spot where she'd last seen him. The minutes ticked past. She strained toward every sound. A rustle. A crack. A thud. Like something heavy falling or… a man hitting the ground.

She sprang to her feet, her heart swelling in her chest so she couldn't get in a breath.

He'd been gone a long time. Had Blackie found him? Found them?

9

Sam dragged the branch he'd broken from the tree back toward their camp. He paused when he saw Yvette. She looked in his direction though not directly at him. Her eyes were wide. Frightened. She held a length of firewood in one hand.

Had Blackie returned?

He stopped in the shelter of the trees and took stock of their surroundings. Peered into the gloom. Did something flicker toward the right? He lowered the branch as quietly as possible and silent as a shadow, edged that direction. His breath whooshed out when he saw it was only swaying bushes.

Still, it paid to be careful. But after another few minutes of waiting and studying, he softly called, "Yvette?"

She jumped and spun toward him. "Sam. Are you alone?" She raised the piece of wood.

"I'm alone." He hurried to her side. "What happened?"

"I heard a thump. I thought…" She dropped the wood and flung herself into his arms. "I thought Blackie had found you." She eased back to look into his eyes. "You're not hurt or anything?"

By *anything*, did she mean was he pleased to have her in his arms? Because the answer was yes. But if she meant did he regret frightening her. The answer was still yes.

"You must have heard me pulling down a dead limb." He held her tight, wanting nothing so much as to hold her—not only in his arms but in his heart—and keep her safe forever. Not that he thought it was possible. She needed him only until they got to safety. After that, she would again see him for what he was. A poor uneducated cowboy.

"I'm so glad Blackie didn't hit you on the head again."

"Me too."

She relaxed but made no move to leave his arms. Which suited him just fine. The fire crackled and he remembered who he was, what he was, and his need to make sure Yvette and the boys were safely taken care of.

He slowly released her. "I need to put more wood on the fire."

She watched him go for the branch. Watched him break it into smaller pieces and throw some lengths on the fire.

The uncertainty in her eyes was his undoing and he returned to her. "Yvette, I will protect you to the best of my ability and do everything in my power to get you and the boys to safety."

Her soft chuckle surprised him. Did she find him amusing?

"I know that without you saying it. Like I said, I trust you."

"Then what is it?"

She shifted to look at the fire. "I'm reluctant to have you out of my sight." Her gaze returned to him, full of silent wishes that he vowed he would do his best to fulfill. "I feel safe when you're here."

He nodded, understanding what she said but wishing for more. More than her security until they reached the fort.

She moved closer until he had no choice but to open his arms and hold her. She sighed softly. Contentedly. Reminded him of an old cat they once had that liked to be petted and would turn all soft and boneless.

"Yvette." But he couldn't say what was in his heart. Didn't have the words. And even if he did, he didn't have the right to say them. "You need to get some sleep. We have to keep up our strength." Although he'd do everything he could to ease things, the journey ahead would be a challenge for Yvette and the boys.

He picked up the blanket that had fallen from

Yvette's shoulders, wrapped it around her and nodded for her to lie down.

"What about you?" she asked.

"I'll rest." Though it would be sitting up with one eye open to make sure Blackie didn't come upon them and catch them all sleeping.

Yvette lay down next to the boys, her face toward him, her eyes open and watchful.

"Go to sleep," he murmured.

"I'm trying."

"Try closing your eyes."

She laughed and lowered her eyelids. Within minutes, he heard her breathing deepen.

Thankfully, she slept. The journey ahead would require endurance from all of them but would be especially hard on Yvette. She was not used to such challenges.

He pulled his blanket around him and sat close to the fire. He'd be adding wood throughout the night even though it would be a clear signal to Blackie as to their whereabouts. Their clothes still damp, they needed heat and also needed to ward off wild animals.

He wakened with a start. The fire blazed, the sky was still dark so he couldn't have slept long. He sat up. And blinked when he saw Yvette across the fire.

"Yvette? Why aren't you sleeping?"

"I knew what you planned. So I decided I would

sleep a few hours then take over watch. So go back to sleep."

He yawned so hard his eyes watered. "How long have you been there?"

"Minutes. Mere minutes. Go back to sleep."

"I'm fine. You rest." How could he have closed his eyes and leave her unguarded?

"Didn't someone say we need to keep up our strength? Hmm. Who would that have been? Oh, I know. You. And I believe it applies as much to you as to me or the children."

He glanced toward the boys, glad to see they were sleeping soundly. "Poor little guys are used to dealing with awful situations."

"It's sad. But you aren't going to divert me. Your turn to sleep." She jabbed her finger toward the place he'd lain.

"Anyone tell you you're bossy?" he murmured.

"Don't believe it's one of the names I've heard to describe me. Now go to sleep." She jabbed her finger again.

"Fine." Smiling, he put his head down. It was rather pleasant to have someone concerned about him. Which was silly. Maude and John and the others cared about him. Grace cared about him.

But believing Yvette cared was a different matter.

. . .

He jerked awake to the sound of wood being put on the fire and opened his eyes to watch Yvette. She certainly looked different than the first time he'd seen her all dolled up, her hair swept up into a fancy style, fixed in place with pearly combs. She'd worn a dress of shiny satin, with a thousand or so ruffles and pearl buttons decorating the bodice.

Like a page out of one of those fashion magazines Grace had brought. As untouchable and unreal as the pictures on the pages.

Now her hair hung down her back in long ringlets. In this light, it appeared black, but he knew it was shiny brown, like a mink he'd once seen. Her dress was wrinkled but more attractive than all the layers of clothing she normally wore.

She hummed quietly as she straightened and looked toward the trees.

He looked too. Neither saw nor heard anything except the breeze sighing through the branches and the rumble of the river.

He returned his gaze to Yvette. Her eyes found his. The air between them shimmered with something he'd never before experienced and had no name for. Nevertheless, it was a welcome sensation, full of hope and promise.

"You're awake." Her words whispered across the distance, echoing in his head that had lost all ability to hold a rational thought.

"Yeah." When had his voice grown so hoarse?

"Light is creeping up the eastern sky."

"Oh."

"Dawn," she said; a hint of amusement in her voice.

Was his confusion so evident? He jumped to his feet, folded his blanket, grabbed the nearest container, and headed for the river to fill it with water.

He paused on the bank overlooking the river and scanned the downstream view. Blackie's hat had washed to the gravel edge. Probably cleaner than it had been in ages. He squinted into trees beside the river. His breathing eased when he didn't see any sign of the man. Nor did he see the horses. It would have been good to have a horse or two as they set out on their journey.

The sky paled as the day began. He scrambled down the bank to the river. Took a few minutes to wash then returned with the metal container full of water.

The boys woke up at his approach. At first, their eyes were wide, startled. When they saw who it was, they each let out a gusty breath.

"Let's have breakfast and get ready to move out." He put as much enthusiasm and excitement in his voice as he could.

The boys ran into the trees to relieve themselves then returned.

"Let's go wash." Yvette took them to the river.

Sam followed to the edge of the clearing where he could watch them. His gaze darted to the trees and then back to Yvette who squatted by the river and splashed water on her face. She said something to the boys and they laughed. Sam smiled. Something about this scene warmed him. Made him almost remember something. Before he could pinpoint the memory, Yvette turned, saw him, and waved, a smile lighting her face.

It wasn't a memory.

It was a dream he remembered.

A recurring dream. The details in his dreams varied. But the feeling was always the same.

The boys scrambled up the bank, faces shiny and eyes bright.

Sam pushed away the threads of that impossible dream and reached out to assist Yvette the last few feet.

She kept hold of his hand as she stood before him, her gaze steady. Her eyes looked into his, seeking, searching, pleading. Pleading? Why would he think that?

It was only a reflection of his own heart that wanted more than he could hope for.

"Let's get breakfast." They returned to camp. Today it would again be peaches and jerky but before the day was out, he would find something else for their evening meal.

They ate quickly.

He didn't want to carry two heavy pack bags, but everything from them was important. Though he could leave behind the ruined food. He held up the heavy coat. It would be useful for Yvette to sleep on but it was still wet. In the end, he left it hanging on a tree.

With a little adjustment, he could carry one side pack like a backpack.

He sent the boys to fetch water to drown the fire and then they were on their way. He led them along the bank that overlooked the river. But he constantly checked to make sure the footing was solid before they moved forward.

Every few steps he glanced over his shoulder to make sure Yvette and the boys were following safely. Yvette had insisted she'd follow the boys. Sam hoped that the path ahead would widen so he could walk beside her.

The trail narrowed even further as the river went around a bend. It was necessary to climb over boulders. Sam stopped at each and waited for the boys and then Yvette to make it safely across and edge around him. It would take only a slip of the foot for one of them to tumble to the rocks below. Or to dash their foot and injure themselves.

Lord, God, give us feet like those of a deer.

He didn't realize he prayed aloud as Yvette gripped his hand and eased to the ground facing him. Her expression filled with determination but her eyes glimmered with something he considered might be pleasure. As soon as the thought surfaced he dismissed it. This journey called for endurance and left room for nothing else.

He edged around her and resumed leading them. The bank flattened and they reached a wide valley with gravel edges by the river. His boots slipped on the rocks. It would be so easy to turn an ankle. He called a stop to catch their breath but in truth, he needed to study their surroundings and see if there was a safer way. A nice path through the grass would be great.

Perhaps if they moved toward the trees…

It was an idea worth exploring. He took one step in that direction when a crashing sound across the river jerked his attention that way.

Something big and clumsy headed their direction.

"Run." The boys didn't need to be told twice. Yvette hesitated as if uncertain what to do. He caught her hand and raced for the shelter of the trees.

YVETTE COULDN'T MAKE her feet work until Sam took her hand and pulled her along.

One word stuck in her throat, almost choking her.

"Blackie?" she managed to whisper. She gathered up the saliva in her mouth and tried to swallow, but all she found was dust and fear.

"I don't know." He pulled her deeper into the trees. The four of them stopped behind some bushes. "Wait here while I check." But she couldn't let him go.

"I'm scared," she murmured.

The boys watched her with big eyes. The way they clutched hands and stood poised to run made her certain they were just as frightened as she.

Sam brought her hands to his chest and pressed the palm of his other hand to her cheek. "I won't leave you. I will protect you. But I need to know what dangers we face."

She clung to his gaze. Drank deeply and freely of the promises flowing from his eyes. Finding courage from what he offered, she nodded.

He slowly lowered his hands and she released her grip. "I'll be right back." He slipped away, clinging to the trees. And then she couldn't see him.

Gil and Tad moved to her side and she pulled them close. Felt tension in their shoulders that matched her own.

The seconds ticked by with maddening slowness.

"Yvette, boys." She startled at Sam's sudden appearance and his whisper. "Come and see." He beckoned them forward.

She wasn't sure she wanted to go. Was it Blackie plotting how to get across the river? Or had he already jumped into the water and even now swam toward them?

Sam reached for her hand. She was powerless to stop herself from lifting it to him.

He drew her through the trees, the boys clinging as close to her back as her next breath.

The trees opened up and they stopped.

She gasped at what she saw—a moose with a rack so wide she wondered how it could carry it. The animal lifted its head and looked around. A flap of skin under its chin waved back and forth. The big brute lowered its muzzle and drank. Lifted its head again and with long-legged ease, loped away.

They stood staring after the animal even when it had disappeared into the trees. It was such a gift when she'd feared Blackie that she chuckled and then had to explain herself to the others.

"It's especially amusing when Sam had mentioned having the feet of a deer. Did you know that's a Bible verse?"

Sam indicated they should move on, but he stayed close to the trees where it was easier walking and he remained at her side.

She continued. "It's a verse in Second Samuel. 'He maketh my feet like hinds' feet: and setteth me upon my high places.' A hind is a type of deer," she explained to the boys who listened to her.

"Do you know lots of verses?" Tad asked.

"I have been learning them. I have discovered they guide me and comfort me. I learned it really well when things didn't go well in my life. Reading my Bible and memorizing verses really helped." She recalled those days of heartache after she'd learned the truth about Morgan.

"Are you referring to your ex-beau?" Sam spoke quietly so the boys wouldn't hear.

She nodded.

"I'm sorry he treated you so poorly."

"Thanks. He used me." Acknowledging the fact no longer sent pain and regret through her veins. "He was a poor specimen of mankind. Not able to see past his own selfish desires. Showing no concern for the well-being of another." The opposite of Sam whom she knew would protect her. Perhaps to his own detriment.

She almost stumbled.

He caught her. "Are you getting tired?"

"Not at all. Just a little clumsy is all." She watched the ground intently as she tried to bring her thoughts back from the fear that raced through her. If Blackie found them, she knew that Sam would fight him, defend her with that knife he carried in the pack. The hilt stuck out so he could grab it quickly. He would not quit until one of them was incapacitated. Blackie was ruthless, without morals. He wouldn't hesitate to kill Sam.

Oh God, I need Your strength and divine courage. Protect us all. Especially Sam.

She'd memorized Psalm One hundred twenty-one that began with 'I will lift up mine eyes unto the hills.' She looked toward the nearby mountain peaks. 'My help cometh from the Lord, which made heaven and earth.' But it was a later verse that comforted her. 'The

Lord shall preserve thee from all evil: He shall preserve thy soul.' God was with them. She would trust Him to protect them.

And if He chose to use Sam as His hands and feet, she didn't mind in the least. So long as they arrived somewhere safe with all Sam's limbs still intact.

They continued on, the river on their right, the trees on their left. In some places, the passageway narrowed, and they had to go single file. At other times, the way was broad, covered with grass. It made for a pleasant walk. Especially when Sam stayed at her side.

There were so many things she wanted to know about him and plied him with questions.

"What was your mother like?"

"She was kind and gentle. My folks were hospitable and often had visitors in, especially on Sundays." He paused as if searching his memories. "I remember sitting on a stool by her chair in the evening. She would read to us. And it was her who first taught me to memorize Bible verses. I sometimes balked at it. But she said that what we filled our hearts and minds with is what we will become. I didn't understand at first, but I guess I do now. I regret that I argued with her about it." His voice deepened. "I fear I was a disappointment to her."

Yvette felt his pain as if she'd been shot with an arrow. She stopped walking and caught his arm. "Sam, no. I can't believe that."

He stilled, then slowly brought his gaze to her. "I was a poor student. I struggled to memorize verses, partly because I didn't want to." He paused, but sensing he had more to say, she waited for him to continue.

"One time the teacher came to speak to Ma. I overheard them. She said I lacked the ability to learn. It was a waste of time to send me to school."

Her heart clenched at the agony in his words. "Sam, I can't believe a teacher would say that. How unkind."

He shrugged. "She only spoke the truth."

"What did your mother say to that?" From what she'd learned from Grace, Yvette understood his parents to be loving and kind. Surely his mother would have said something to counteract those words.

His gaze slowly returned to her, but it didn't connect. "I don't remember."

"Try. I think it's important that you do."

He shook his head. "It doesn't matter. A cowboy doesn't need to be able to write beautiful prose. Especially if he has a friend who will write his letters for him." He gave a laugh that was entirely mirthless. "The boys are getting ahead of us."

She allowed him to hurry her along the path, not wanting to be too far behind the children, but her thoughts spun. What could she say to comfort him?

But Sam kept them going at a steady pace for the

next couple of hours. The rugged trail required she concentrate on where she put her feet.

Tad sat down and whimpered.

Gil urged him to get up. "We got to keep going."

But Tad pushed his brother away.

She and Sam rushed to his side. She knelt beside the child. "What's wrong?" Besides the obvious. They were tired and hungry and likely lost. But he hadn't complained previously.

For an answer, Tad looked at her with tear-filled eyes, full of pleading that tore at her heart. She gathered him into her arms.

"Oh, Tad. I know you're hungry and tired."

The midday sun was warm, but it didn't begin to account for the heat of Tad's little body. She touched his forehead. "He's fevered."

Sam knelt beside her and felt Tad's face. "He's hot." He sat back and rubbed his neck. "What do you think we should do?"

It was nice that he thought she should know. "Whenever I was sick, my parents brought in a doctor. Do you think we should send for one?"

He jerked his gaze to her and laughed. "You and I will have to do. We'll have to stop here for the day and take care of him. I'll scout around and find a good camping place." He was gone before Yvette could admit she didn't like to have him out of her sight.

Gil pressed to her side. "Is he going to die?"

She wrapped an arm around him. "I hope not. But

he needs to rest until he's feeling better." Though they could carry him out. She looked at the backpack Sam had left on the ground. Could she carry it and let Sam carry Tad? It would slow them immensely and use strength she feared would dissipate before they reached safety.

If only they could come across one of the horses.

Sam returned. "There's a sheltered spot over here." He took Tad from Yvette. The little boy moaned at being disturbed.

Yvette reached for the backpack, discovered it to be heavier than she expected, but she hoisted it to her shoulder and followed Sam and Gil.

The little clearing Sam had chosen was grassy. Conifer and deciduous trees surrounded it. The scent of pine and mountain air filled her nostrils. Apart from present circumstances, it would have been a pleasant place to spend an afternoon.

She dropped the pack, opened it, and took out a blanket to spread for Tad to rest on. Sam laid him down. Tad curled up into a ball, clutching his stomach and moaning.

Yvette knelt at his side, stroking his brow and making hushing noises.

Sam took a knee at her side. "I'm guessing he drank too much river water."

"I thought it was safe to drink from the river."

"It is. But perhaps something in the bushes where

they were." He shrugged. "I really don't know. But he's not in any shape to travel."

"So what do we do?" She watched him, expecting him to have an answer.

He held her gaze, steady and reassuring. "We'll take care of him with what we have."

"Which is two cans of peaches and some beans."

"You forget we also have water and prayer." He signaled Gil to his side and took Yvette's hand. "Nothing is impossible with God." He bowed his head. "Our Father in heaven, help Tad to get better. Show us what to do. Protect us. For thine is the kingdom, the power, and the glory, forever. Amen."

She sat still, letting the peace of God bless her, thanks to Sam's faith and prayer.

He slipped his hand away and pushed to his feet. "I'll get water. We need to sponge him to get the fever down and he needs to drink if he can." He took a container from the backpack and trotted toward the river.

Gil pressed to Yvette's side. "Sam knows what to do, doesn't he?"

"I believe he does."

"He'll take care of Tad and us."

She hugged Gil. "Do you think God brought Sam with us to help us?" She certainly did and thanked Him for doing so.

"Sure do." Gil rested against her, reassured at her words.

Sam returned. He handed the container of water to Yvette. "You sponge him while I get a fire going."

Gil looked from Yvette to Sam, then followed Sam to help find wood.

From the backpack, she took the underskirt she'd stuck in this morning and tore a portion from it, dipped it in water and gently wiped at Tad's face.

He groaned a protest.

She murmured words of comfort as she continued.

Sam and Gil returned and built the fire, then Sam sat at her side.

"Sam, I don't mind admitting that I have no experience with sick children. I'm glad you're here and know what to do."

"I learned a few things in the orphanage. Not all good. But there was one grandma-type woman who came in to help several days a week. When we weren't feeling well, we were always glad to see her. She was so gentle and kind. I still remember the touch of her hand on my forehead when I had the measles."

At the catch in his voice, she squeezed his hand. "I'm glad there was someone there to comfort you. Just as I'm so very grateful you are here to take care of us."

She felt him stiffen.

"You'd do fine without me."

She knew he meant to be dismissive. Guessed he wasn't used to being told he was appreciated for anything but being a cowboy. "Sam, I wouldn't have a clue what to do. If I have to be stranded out in the middle of nowhere, I'm grateful that it's with you."

"Someone like me, you mean."

"Not someone like you. You. No one but you."

The air between them shimmered with the meaning of her words. Yes, Pete, or Adam, or Maude could have been with her and helped her, but it wouldn't have been the same. There was something special about Sam. Something that made her know she was safe. That thought wormed its way into her heart and settled there like it meant to take up permanent residence.

And she welcomed it.

His hand tightened around hers but he didn't say anything. After a heartbeat of waiting and hoping, he rose. "I'll get water to drink." And he was gone.

Her heart stalled. Refused to beat. She knew he hadn't abandoned her and yet she felt alone and empty without him. It was an unfamiliar feeling.

"He said he would get us something to eat," Gil said, his tone a mixture of worry and assurance.

"Is there a store hiding nearby?" she asked, knowing there wasn't but wanting to make Gil relax.

He giggled. "If there was could I have a candy stick?"

"Sweetie, if there was, I'd buy a whole sack of candy for you and your brother."

Gil looked at her with such adoration, she felt bigger and stronger than she was.

"You would?"

"Yes, and new clothes for all of us." She looked at her wrinkled skirt and shirtwaist.

"You must be very rich," he said with awe.

Rich? She looked past the boy. Beyond the present. Into the past with the hurts of being treated differently because of her father's money. She blinked and thought of the future. One where money didn't factor so largely in her life…her happiness.

She brought her gaze back to Gil. "I have more than enough." It wasn't money she even meant. She hugged Gil. "I have friends like you and Tad and Sam. That's worth more than money."

She resumed sponging Tad.

The minutes ticked past. Tad stirred and moaned.

Where was Sam? He'd been gone far too long.

The skin on the back of Yvette's neck twitched with the feeling someone watched her.

10

Taken in by the scene ahead of him, Sam stopped before he reached the others. A fire burning. A little boy sleeping at one side. Another sitting cross-legged, looking up at the woman. The beautiful woman washing a cool rag over one boy and saying something to the other that earned her a smile.

It was another reminder of his recurring dream.

Yvette lifted her head and sat very still. As if she felt his presence.

He moved forward. "Got us dinner." He held up the two fish he'd caught.

Gil and Yvette looked at him in surprise.

She squinted. "How did you get them? Do you just call and they jump into your arms?"

He chuckled at her question. "I told you, Maude made sure we could survive if we got stranded somewhere." He would thank her from the depths of his heart when he saw her again.

"No, seriously, how did you do that?"

He pulled out a flat pan that would serve for frying the fish. "Wish I had a cast-iron frying pan but then I'd have to carry it, wouldn't I? How is Tad?"

"He's less restless but still curls up with cramps." She turned from looking at the boy to give Sam a hard look. "About the fish…"

"I'll fry them. They'd be better if I had flour and salt to dip them in but I don't."

She narrowed her eyes. "Is it a federal secret as to how you caught them?"

He got the pan hot. The fish were cleaned and ready to fry. At Yvette's question, he looked up, pretending to be startled. "Well, I never thought of it but perhaps it's Maude's secret."

Yvette let out a long-suffering sigh. "Fine. I'll ask Maude when I see her."

He chuckled. "I tied my pocketknife to a branch and speared the fish."

"So that's why you took some of the rope from the pack." She looked suitably impressed. "Is it hard?"

"You have to account for how the water bends where you see the fish." He dropped the pieces of fish to the hot pan. As he had no grease, he would need to stir it constantly to keep it from sticking.

"Can you teach me?"

His hand stilled and he looked at her eager face. A

smile started in the pit of his stomach as he imagined her trying to spear a fish. The smile spread to his mouth and warmed his eyes. "Might be kind of fun."

Her brows rose. "Why are you grinning so widely?"

He shrugged. "Just remembering when I learned."

She nodded and turned back to Tad. His eyes were open and he watched them. She pressed a hand to his forehead. "How are you feeling?"

"My tummy hurts."

"I think your fever has gone down. How about a drink?"

Sam had brought water and she offered him some.

He sipped a little then lay down. "I'm tired."

Sam reached over and stroked Tad's forehead. "You rest. We'll stay here until you're feeling better." He kept his hand on Tad's forehead until the boy closed his eyes and relaxed. "I think he's on the mend," he murmured. "But I don't intend to push him."

The fish was ready and he divided it among the three of them. He wasn't the only one who ate slowly and thoughtfully. The sooner they moved on, the sooner they'd reach safety. But he feared if he tried to make Tad travel at this time, the boy would get worse rather than better. They were safe enough here. He could get fish for them. They had water. And fuel for a fire.

And good company.

His heart smote him. He had no right to be rejoicing over spending time with Yvette and the boys.

They needed him to get them to safety. Not to selfishly enjoy having them to himself. But he knew that once they got back, Yvette would return to her family, or—the thought felt like he'd swallowed a fish bone and it'd stuck in his throat—write to some dude with a view to marrying him.

Groaning, Tad turned to his other side. He clutched his tummy.

It wasn't selfish to be concerned about the boy's wellbeing.

The simple meal was over. He let the fire die down for now. They wouldn't need the heat until later in the day.

"I'm going to have a look around." But before he took a step, Yvette was on her feet.

"Where are you going? How long will you be?"

He caught her hand and pulled her close, looking down into her hazel eyes. He brushed a strand of her hair off her cheek, resisting the temptation to let his fingers linger on the soft skin.

"I won't be long."

"What are you looking for?"

He heard the worry in her voice and smiled assurance. "Nothing. Unless there is a ranch house nearby."

"You think there is?"

"No, Yvette. But it's only smart to check out our surroundings."

She nodded. "Of course." Her gaze never left his.

"I'll be back."

Her smile faltered, but she patted his arm. "I'm counting on it."

He didn't move. Couldn't. His feet seemed to have grown roots. Bits of his dream flitted through his head. A woman who needed him, wanted him. Waited for his return.

He shook his head to drive away the wisps of that dream and strode into the trees. He made widening circles around their camp making sure no dangers threatened them. He found nothing but some wild raspberries which he planned to return to and pick for supper. His journey took him back to the river where he hunkered down to wait and watch. Where was Blackie? Had he been injured in the fall? Was he stretched out nearby needing help? Not that Sam wanted to aid the man, but John and Maude's teaching was embedded in his mind. How often had he heard the words in one form or another, but mostly a direct quote from the Bible? *Be not overcome of evil, but overcome evil with good.*

Yes, he acknowledged with a deep sigh, if he saw Blackie needing help, he would offer it. But he saw nothing to indicate Blackie needed help or was searching for them. It seemed he should have joined them again by now. God willing, he had decided it wasn't worth the effort. Sam would continue to watch for the man, but for now, they were free of him.

He returned to the berries, made a basket with his

shirt tail, picked all the ripe ones, then made his way back to camp.

Yvette smiled a welcome that settled into the corners of his heart. Her gaze went to the way he held his shirt. She rose to watch him approach.

He stopped in front of her. "Berries," he said.

It seemed to him that she clung to his gaze as if she didn't want to leave off looking at him. He swallowed hard. Remembered the fruit he carried. He took one and held it to her lips.

Still holding his gaze, she opened her mouth and took the berry from his fingers.

He looked longingly at the bit of red staining her lips.

She sucked the juicy fruit.

He knew when the flavor hit her taste buds. Her eyes widened, brimmed with pleasure.

"Those are delicious. Give them to the boys."

"Wouldn't hurt you to enjoy them too." He held another to her lips, pleased when she again took it from his fingers. Not that he could explain why it mattered. Except it did.

She sighed her pleasure at the burst of flavor on her tongue. Her eyes still held his, drawing him in, though neither of them moved. It was her heart he moved toward. Or was it *his* heart she moved toward? He didn't know and didn't want to think about it too deeply lest it bring an end to this moment that overflowed with possibility.

Gil shifted, the rustling sound jerking Sam to his senses. Just because he'd felt his dream so vividly a few times was no reason to forget he was a penniless cowboy. Well, maybe not exactly penniless, but in comparison to Yvette's family, his belongings were mighty unremarkable.

"Would you like some berries?" he asked, forcing himself to turn from Yvette.

Gil took some, but before he popped them into his mouth, he asked, "You think Tad could eat some?"

"Let's see." Sam hunkered down beside Tad. The boy opened his eyes but struggled to focus them. His eyelids fluttered as if he wanted to go back to sleep.

Gil knelt over his little brother. "We got raspberries. You want some?"

Tad groaned and clutched at his stomach then rolled away to show them his back.

"His stomach is still too upset." Sam pressed his hand to Gil's back to reassure him.

"He's improving," Yvette murmured and reached for Gil's back at the same time as Sam did. Their hands brushed together. Warmth flowed up his arm. His dream grew clearer.

Knowing it was impossible, he drew his hand back. Pulled his wayward thoughts into submission.

Yvette sat back on her heels and looked at him, then lowered her gaze, but not before he saw that his sudden withdrawal had hurt her.

Perhaps there was a way he could erase that. "Are you still wanting to learn how to fish?"

"Indeed." She erased every regret in his heart with her beaming smile. Then it slipped sideways. "What about Tad?"

"We'll take him with us. He can rest and watch." He forced his eyes from Yvette to Tad. "Is that all right, little guy?"

Tad managed to give a slight nod.

Sam studied the boy a moment. He looked mighty poorly, but there was little they could do for him other than let him rest. He scooped Tad up. At least he wasn't still hot.

"Gil, bring the things." He nodded toward where he'd left his makeshift spear.

They went to the river. Sam led them to the spot where he'd found good fishing and laid Tad in the shade. "You rest."

Yvette hovered at his shoulder as he made sure the boy was comfortable. He straightened slowly, not wanting her to back away. Just as slowly, he turned to face her.

She took her time about lifting her gaze from Tad to him.

Something filled the air between them. Something as sweet as the raspberries they'd enjoyed. As warm as the overhead sun. As fresh as the water tumbling by. And full of hope and promises and wishes.

Her throat worked as she swallowed.

Did that mean she was as aware as he of the tension crowding against them? It made him want to open his arms and hold her to his chest as he had done when they escaped the river. But he had no such excuse this time.

"I see fish," Gil called, making Sam remember what he was supposed to be doing.

He reluctantly left Yvette—he met Tad—and went to the river. Rather than use the spear he'd fashioned with his pocketknife, he showed them how to make spears from a green branch. He let each of them sharpen the point themselves, then gave instructions on how to stab a fish. "The tricky part is taking into account how the water bends what you see. We'll practice on clumps of grass until you figure it out." He moved away from where fish could be seen and dropped some lumps into the water. "Let's see how you do."

Gil stabbed at the target. Missed.

Yvette eyed her target for several minutes. "I have to take into account the refraction of the water." She edged her spear into the water and eyeballed the bend. She pulled it from the water and aimed it at a different angle. After doing that four times, she nodded, lifted the spear and jabbed it at the lump of grass. She missed and was so surprised, she almost tumbled in after it.

She jerked back and gave Sam a look of such annoyance that he grinned.

"Don't laugh. It's hard."

He sobered, though his insides continued to hold a wide smile. "I know it. I had to learn."

"Well, if you can do it, I can do it." She spoke through gritted teeth.

He stilled. Her words were different, but the message was the same—he was a dumb bloke. Anyone could outsmart, out learn, out spear him.

"I'm not surprised you think that."

YVETTE DREW BACK at the tone of Sam's voice. Had she said something that offended him? She reviewed her words and groaned. "I didn't say if you could learn it must be easy. Sam. Really. I meant I am not going to give up any more than you did to learn this." She was rewarded by the way the tension disappeared from around his mouth. "Watch. I am going to spear it this time." She figured she was a few degrees off so she only had to correct her aim by those few degrees and she'd be successful.

She raised her arm over her head and gave a warrior cry such as she'd heard young men as they prepared to play some sport. It sounded nothing like the whooping of a dozen sports fanatics, but still, it signified her determination and she thrust her spear down, carrying through with her whole body.

Only she missed the lump of dirt and nothing

stopped her body from following her arm. She flailed her arms and gave a cry that was anything but strong and challenging. In fact, she might have sounded something like a strangled chicken. She was going to get wet and she was tired of getting wet.

But it wasn't the river she fell into. It was Sam's strong arms.

"Whoa there. No point in you swimming after fish." He staggered back.

She feared they would both end up in the water.

But he twisted and they fell to the gravelly shore, his arms around her, pressing her shoulder hard to his chest. Air whooshed from his lungs.

They lay sprawled on the rocky ground. Her heart beat out a war cry of its own, harsh and insistent. She was stuck on her back like an upside-down beetle.

He shifted, tried to free his arm by turning away. That didn't work. He turned toward her. "I'm stuck," he said.

She wriggled.

He pulled. Reached across her. Planted his hand at her side and lifted. His face was above hers. His blue eyes flashing like the water rushing by their feet. His gaze was steady, watchful. He has the good beginnings of a beard. Whiskers as blond as sunshine.

The moment seemed frozen in time.

Then he shifted. "You'll have to excuse me, but it's the only way for me to get up." He pushed to his knees and was over top of her, but before she could even think of how close he was, he was on his feet and reaching down to help her up.

He studied her face, ran his hands up and down her arms. "No injuries?"

Swallowing hard, she ran her hands up and down her arms. "No injuries."

He smiled. "No fish either." He stepped away and retrieved her spear. "Ready to give up, little rich girl?"

She wrinkled her nose at him. "Never." She tossed her head. "Maude is right. You never know when you might need to know this. Say for instance, if—heaven forbid—something happens to you, I need to be able to get food for us."

He narrowed the distance separating them and leaned close. "Do you foresee me being injured?"

She tried to maintain her teasing, but his eyes held hers, made it impossible to think. She touched his cheek. "I'm sorry for even joking about it. I'm counting on you to get us to safety."

He caught her hand and pressed it to his face. "Then no more tackling me and trying to drown me in the river."

She sputtered. "I never..." saw the twinkle in his eyes... "If I'd wanted to push you in the river, I would have succeeded." And to prove the point, she gave him a little shove.

He backed up and lost his balance. He flailed his arms. And was about to end up in the water.

She grabbed his hands and dragged him back.

"Had you worried there, didn't I?" He tipped his head back and roared with laughter.

"You. You." She reached for him but he darted away. She picked up her skirt and raced after him. But he jumped from side to side, always just out of her reach until she was laughing so hard she couldn't breathe. She stopped and leaned over her knees.

He stopped too, leaning back on his heels. Staying far enough away she couldn't catch him. Not that she could remember what she meant to do if she did.

It was supposed to be to punish him for something he'd done, but all she could think was if she caught him, his punishment might be to kiss her.

But she didn't want a kiss from him to be punishment.

Oh, what was wrong with her that she couldn't think clearly?

11

"I got one," Gil hollered, bringing Sam's thoughts back to where they belonged—on teaching these two to fish. Like Yvette said, they never knew when they might need the skill. Hopefully not in his lifetime.

He and Yvette checked on Tad. He rested, his eyes on the activities around him but his knees still drawn up to his stomach. Seeing he was all right, they hurried back to Gil. He'd speared the lump of dirt and held it aloft.

"Good boy. Now it's time to catch a fish." He led them to a still spot where fish idled and explained how to keep their shadow off the water. "You get one chance and then you'll have to wait for the fish to calm down or find another spot. Are you ready?"

Gil nodded.

"Careful of your angle."

"I got it figured out." The boy hovered by the edge

of the water, still as a rock, and waited for a fish to get to the place where he seemed to think he had his best chance.

Sam held his breath, silently cheering for the boy. Gil moved with a quickness that surprised and startled Sam then hoisted his spear, with a fish on its tip.

"I did it! I did it!"

"You sure did." Sam patted the boy's back.

Yvette congratulated him. "Now I have to do it." She returned to where she'd been practicing and slowly lowered the spear, once, twice, three times. "I've got it." With a snap of her wrist, she jabbed the lump of dirt and lifted it. "Now for a fish." She marched to the spot where Gil had been successful and poised herself as Gil had.

She drew in slow, steady breaths.

"You think she can do it?" Gil whispered.

"I kind of think she can do anything she makes up her mind to do," Sam whispered back.

He knew Yvette had heard him when she grinned in his direction. Then she returned her attention to her task.

A moment later, she jabbed her spear.

He chuckled at the look on her face as the spear met flesh and then she lifted the fish in the air as Gil had done.

Sam clapped. "So we eat fish for supper."

Yvette slipped her hand through the crook of Sam's elbow. "Can I cook it?"

"Thought you'd never ask. But first, it has to be scaled and cleaned. Come, I'll show you both how to do it."

"Wait a minute. Isn't there some kind of rule that says if one catches it, the other cleans it?"

"Don't remember hearing that rule earlier today when I caught fish." He knelt near a rock that would serve as a table and palmed the bigger knife.

She sighed with resignation. "Have you forgotten I'm a rich girl? Used to having things done for me?"

He rose to his full height, relieved to see the sparkle in her eyes that said she was teasing.

He flicked his finger on her nose. "Have you forgotten that you never know when you might need to know this sort of stuff?"

"Oh, very well. Show me what to do."

They knelt by the rock, Gil at their side with his fish. She sat back on her heels to watch.

"You aren't going to trick me into doing it for you."

Her cheeky grin informed him she might have been considering exactly that.

He continued. "I'll tell you what to do." He instructed both Yvette and Gil on how to prepare their fish for cooking. "There you go. It wasn't that hard was it?"

"I feel like a real pioneer," Yvette said, her eyes glowing with triumph.

"I think there might be more to pioneering than catching and cleaning a fish."

"I believe I could do whatever it took."

He couldn't look away from her steady gaze and in the depths of her eyes, he saw her determination. Knew that it was important to acknowledge her capabilities in this direction. Understood with water-bright clarity that it meant a great deal to her to prove to herself and others that she wasn't just a rich girl.

"I don't doubt it for a minute," he said. "And if anyone thinks having a rich father makes you weak and pampered, they need their eyes fixed."

She lowered her gaze. "Thank you." The words almost disappeared on the breeze.

"You're welcome." He squeezed her shoulder. "And I mean it."

Her head came up. Her eyes flashed. Warmth filled them until he felt it on his skin. "Sam, I think you are the smartest man I've ever met."

"What? Me?" No one had ever called him smart and for good reason.

"Yup. You know all sorts of things that are far more important than book learning. How to catch fish without a rod and hook. How to take care of silly city girls—"

He opened his mouth to protest but she put two fingers on his lips to stop him.

"I expect you know how to rope and ride and take care of cows and horses. But the most telling is you recognize how capable I am." She laughed low and husky.

He caught her hand and pulled it from his lips. "Guess that does make me smart." He wanted to say so much more. But he had no right to say what lay in his heart. They were in a time out of time. When they returned to their normal lives, things would be so much different.

Acknowledging that fact made him turn to Tad. He knelt by the boy. "How are you, little guy? Your tummy still hurt?"

Tad nodded. "I gotta go." He struggled to his feet.

Sam scooped him up and headed for the trees where Tad emptied his bowels. Surely that meant the upset was passing through his body. He carried Tad to the river and cleaned him up then joined Gil and Yvette back at the campsite.

The smile she gave him made his chest expand against the fabric of his shirt. All because he helped a little boy? Or was it because he'd said she was more than a rich girl? Not in so many words but that's what he meant.

They were busy the next couple hours, working together as if born to do so. Tad made several more trips to the bushes. They prepared warm water for him to drink, fried the fish, gave Tad peaches to eat. Sam didn't think the boy's innards would handle fish very well. They washed dishes and helped the boys prepare for bed.

Dusk fell. The boys curled up in blankets by the fire.

"Can you tell us a story?" Tad asked.

Sam wasn't sure which adult they meant and nodded toward Yvette. "Go ahead."

"Very well but why don't we take turns?" She took his agreement for granted and began to talk. "Once upon a time there were two little boys lost in the woods. They were hungry…." She spun a tale that was very much like their present circumstances only the boys were brave and resourceful and discovered a cabin where a kind man and woman lived who ended up adopting the boys. "And they lived happily ever after."

Silence followed. Sam could feel Gil and Tad's yearning for a similar end to their present story. The boys needed a loving set of parents.

"Sam, your turn." Yvette's soft voice jolted him from his thoughts.

"I don't have a story to match yours."

She nudged him with her elbow. "But it will be your story." Her voice softened as she continued. "It will be you."

The lump in his throat at her words made it impossible for him to speak. He swallowed hard, forcing it down. Did she really want to know about *him*? Sure sounded like it.

So he told about how he and Adam had decided to climb up a steep rock embankment. "We climbed side by side. Neither of us said so, but it was a race to see who could get to the top first. We were halfway up when I couldn't find a finger hold to keep climbing. I thought I better go down. But when I reached my foot out to find a toe hold I couldn't find one. So there I was, glued to that rock face." He stopped. The boys were up on their elbows staring at him with wide eyes. "Maybe that isn't a good bedtime story." He sat back, with no intention of finishing.

"Sam!" Yvette grabbed his arm. "You can't leave us with you hanging."

He laughed at her choice of words. "Well, it's obvious I got down because here I am."

"We want to know how you got up or down, don't we boys?"

"Yes," they answered in unison.

"Adam rescued me. He was almost to the top when he saw my problem and he called down that there was a little ledge to my right. I just had to reach for it. I did and with Adam calling instructions, I made it to the top. And here I am." He held out his arms.

Gil sank back with a loud gush of exhaled air. "Whew, I was scared for a minute."

"I wasn't," Tad said. "I knew he would figure out a way. He's so smart."

Yvette chuckled softly and pressed her hand to his arm. "They agree with me."

The boys were soon asleep. Sam signaled Yvette to join him a distance away from them so they could talk.

He wanted to say something about the boys, but what? He couldn't offer them a home other than one at the Circle A Ranch where there were plenty of people to love and care for them. No doubt Blackie would have something to say about that, though more and more he wondered if Blackie had survived. He might give up on his plans for Yvette, but Sam couldn't see him leaving that bundle of money behind. Yvette had said her father would pay a lawyer to make sure the boys went with her. But then Gil and Tad would go to some city and he'd never see them again.

"I've grown fond of the boys." He kept his tone even, revealing none of the turmoil inside his chest.

"Me too. They're a wonderful pair. I'm glad Tad seems to be on the mend. Will he be ready to move on in the morning, do you think?"

"We might have to slow our pace, but I think so."

"Good. I keep thinking of that verse in the Bible. You probably know it too. 'What man of you, having a hundred sheep, if he lose one of them, doth not leave the ninety and nine in the wilderness, and go after that which is lost, until he finds it? And when he hath found it, he layeth it on his shoulders, rejoicing.' I think Gil and Tad are two lost sheep that God has sent us to rescue."

"Umm." What was he to say? There was only one way he and Yvette could take care of the boys. The idea of marrying Yvette and taking in the pair would be the fulfillment of his dream. But reality would take over once they were back in their normal surroundings. Unless—

She continued speaking, saving Sam from wandering too far into his dream. "It's nice that Maude and John have Sunday services and are such strong believers. God had His hand on you when he arranged for you to find a home there."

"I agree."

"You know who you are and what you want." She sounded envious.

If only she knew.

She continued. "You know, out here is the first time I've ever felt…I don't even know. Whole maybe. Important maybe."

"Of course you're important and not just here."

"No, I'm the daughter of a rich man, a valued guest at important occasions, someone who might lend their presence and pledge money to worthy causes. And if you are to believe what is said, everyone's cause is worthy." She paused, but before he could think of anything to say and really, what could he say, she continued.

"After I learned the truth about Morgan, I retreated to my room. I was tired of being an asset to causes, of being a meal ticket for someone else's dreams. I felt drawn to my Bible. I read the Psalms over and over until I knew many of them by heart and then I read other parts of the Bible." She shifted to look directly at him. "I know I am valuable in God's sight. That should be enough." She turned away.

"What else do you need?" He struggled to get the words off his tongue. He wanted to be what she needed, what she wanted. But he had nothing to offer her.

For a moment, she didn't speak, and he wondered if she meant to answer his question. Then she released a long breath.

"I need to be me."

"Who else could you be?"

She didn't move. He wondered if she even breathed.

He touched her arm, surprised when she jumped as if she'd forgotten he was there. "Yvette, I can't imagine anyone wanting you to be anyone else, anything but who you are."

"Thank you." The words whispered in the wind.

They sat for a time in silence. He couldn't tell what she was thinking but knew he'd failed to convince her that she was important in her own right.

She shifted. "If I could have anything I wanted, be anywhere I chose, and be who I long to be, I would marry a man who cared nothing for my father's money." She turned so sharply to face him that he startled. "But how am I to find that unless I'm not honest about being a Bellamy?"

Yvette stared into Sam's eyes. In the dusk of the evening, it was hard to read them. But she felt him waiting. Likely wondering how to answer her questions. They were rhetorical, of course.

His expression shifted. If she could impose her wishes on him, she would say he looked tender, gentle.

"Yvette, how could a man trust you if you presented yourself falsely? I think what you are looking for are truth and trust. And you must give it to receive it."

His answer was profound. Stilled her worries. Gave her hope. "How will I find such a thing?"

"The only thing I can say is trust God. Ask Him to direct you. Doesn't He promise to guide us?"

"Yes, He does." She filled her heart with the assurance his words carried. "Thank you."

They sat shoulder to shoulder watching the moonlight dance on the tumbling water. "Sam, I told you my dream. What's yours?"

If her shoulder hadn't been against his, she wouldn't have felt him stiffen and then slowly relax. Was his dream so strong that it sent a jolt through him?

"What makes you think I have a dream?" he asked.

"I believe we all do whether or not we acknowledge it."

"You're sure of that?"

"Sam, I know you want me to think you don't have

a dream." She leaned her head on his shoulder. "I know you do. I'd like to hear it."

"Why?"

His blunt word was like a spear point to her heart.

"Because I care about you."

Again, that stiffening and then easing. She suspected that he forced himself to relax. To convince himself as well as her, that he didn't hear and react to her words.

"Sam, what dream catches you in the predawn light? Lingers like wisps of fog in the back of your brain, floating to the surface at unexpected times?"

Still no answer.

She waited, feeling in her inner being the crumbling of his resistance.

"I do have a dream," he murmured. "An impossible one."

"Nothing is impossible."

"Flying is impossible. Breathing underwater is impossible. Becoming a giant is impossible."

Despite her disappointment in his refusal to tell her his dream, she laughed. "Trust you to refute my statement."

"Trust, is it?"

"Well, it's not the kind of trust that you meant earlier, but it's still a kind of trust. After all, doesn't trust grow with knowledge?"

"I suppose so." He drew in a long breath. "I think

we should get some sleep. Who knows what tomorrow holds?"

"You're right." Neither of them moved.

"Aren't you tired?" he asked.

"Aren't you?" He'd stayed awake a good portion of last night. He'd carried them all from the river. "Of course you are. How selfish of me to prevent you from going to sleep." She bolted to her feet.

He rose too and took her arm. "You weren't keeping me up. I've enjoyed visiting with you."

She tucked his words into her heart as she rolled up in her blanket. Knowing he slept nearby—or stayed awake to guard them—she knew she was safe, and slept.

S<small>HE WAKENED</small> the next morning and looked into Tad's eyes as he sat cross-legged at her side.

"How are you feeling?" she asked.

"Hungry. You gonna make breakfast?"

"Where's Sam?" She sat up, saw him asleep across the fire from her. His eyes opened and he met her gaze. At the softness in his look, she swallowed hard. It was like a long-distance hug.

Then he sat up. "Looks like morning has arrived." He got the fire going, grabbed a container and went for water.

Yvette would have liked to do something. Cook a

big breakfast for them all. Not that she knew how to cook many things, but she could learn.

She could learn anything if she set her mind to it.

Carrying that thought with her, she poked through the backpack, hoping for something to cook. She hoped in vain.

Sam returned with water and two fish. "I'm beginning to feel like that little boy in the Bible. Except he had five loaves."

Yvette swallowed back a mouthful of saliva as she recalled fresh bread.

He fried the fish and divided it among them. Even Tad wanted some. They shared the rest of the peaches and then packed up.

For a time, they were able to walk on a grassy bank, but it soon gave way to rugged rock overhangs and they climbed up and continued onward a distance from the river.

Yvette gave her surroundings a hard look. Where was Blackie? She wasn't quite ready to believe the man had given up on them.

Tad seemed to be back to his normal energy level and the boys dashed in and out of the trees in some sort of game.

They found more raspberries to enjoy and then Sam helped her and the boys down a slope to the bushes and introduced her to a new berry—the saskatoon berry.

"Most of the fruit is overripe, but we can find a few to eat," he explained. He plucked three from the bushes and offered them to Yvette, holding them toward her lips.

Remembering how his touch had affected her when he had done the same with raspberries, she wondered if it was wise to repeat the experience. But her mouth opened as if it didn't hear her thoughts.

His fingers touched her lips, sending a flood of warmth directly to her heart.

She crunched on the berries. They were nothing like she expected. Nutty, almond flavor with a touch of sweet juice.

"Good aren't they?" he asked, reaching for more berries.

The boys were eating them.

She didn't move for a moment as she watched Sam and the boys.

This was the life she wanted. Only with a house—a small house. Like Sam said, an impossible dream. Her father would whisk her back home if—when—they reached the fort. Sam would continue being a cowboy.

But a cowboy could have a wife and family.

And a rich girl could persuade her father to let her live the life she wanted.

And she could dream impossible dreams.

12

Sam was concerned about Tad eating too many of the berries. They might go straight through him and trigger cramps.

"Let's keep moving." The boys scampered up the hill. Sam took Yvette's hand and pulled her after him. He paused at the top to let her catch her breath and arrange her skirt.

She finished and looked up at him. "I'm a real mess, aren't I?"

He ran his gaze slowly up and down her length, every inch replacing with softness and light the hardness in his heart that he'd been unaware of. When did it get there and how?

He realized she waited for him to answer. "You look ready to handle whatever comes your way."

Her pleased smile informed him that his words

meant much to her. Knowing he had given her something she valued further eased life into his heart.

The boys laughed at something, reminding him of his task to see these people to safety.

He and Yvette caught up to the boys.

They stopped at noon for some beef jerky. Not exactly what a boy with a stomach upset should eat, but there weren't many options. Their short rations made it even more important that they keep moving. He allowed half an hour of rest then they continued.

The sun grew hot overhead. He led them down a rocky incline to the river where they could drink and splash the cooling water over their faces.

They didn't go much further before Tad started dragging his feet. The little guy didn't complain, but it was obvious he was exhausted.

"I'll carry you." Sam shucked the backpack off and knelt down so Tad could climb on his back. He was about to pick up the pack and carry it in his hands when Yvette took it and tried to put it on her back.

"You don't need to do that," he said.

"I can do my share."

"Seems to me you have been. Have you forgotten the fish?" He hoped his tone was teasing while he struggled to think of her carrying that weight.

"Help me." Her words were half plea, half order. She must have sensed his hesitation. "Please. Sam, I'm tired of being pampered."

"Pampered?" He roared with laughter which shook

Tad, making him giggle. "If being shut up in a little cabin, being tossed into a river, almost drowning, and then surviving on fish and berries is your idea of being pampered, I don't think I want to know what you consider a hardship."

She chuckled. "Probably best if we don't find out. Now, are you going to help me or not?"

He decided there wasn't any point in arguing with her and helped her adjust the pack on her back. The ropes would cut into her shoulders and she would soon find the weight a challenge, but he wondered if she would admit it.

He led the way with Tad on his back and Gil running ahead. Sam continually turned to make sure Yvette was all right until she said, "Sam, I'm not going to fall down. Trust me to do this."

"Fine, but does that trust include you letting me know when you've had enough?"

She had been leaning forward to counter the weight of the backpack but straightened and looked him full in the eyes.

He watched the struggle in her gaze as she fought her need to prove herself with his request to admit when the pack grew too heavy. She sighed loud and long. "You're carrying Tad. It only seems fair for me to carry this."

Fine. If she wasn't going to admit when she'd had enough, he would simply keep an eye on her and decide for himself.

They reached a place where they could walk side by side. Despite his growing urgency to get to the fort, he slowed his steps so she could keep up. Sometime later, she began to stagger. He stopped.

"I'll take that now." He reached for the ropes to slip it from her shoulders.

She caught his hands.

He guessed she meant to stop him. But enough was enough. He waited, silently letting her know he wouldn't let her refuse.

"I can walk now," Tad said and slid from Sam's back.

Sam shifted the pack to his own back and stood studying Yvette. Saw the weariness in her eyes. He touched her cheek. Guessed the way she leaned into his hand indicated how tired she was. "We can stop here."

She straightened. "Not for me. I can keep going."

"Good. We need to get to the fort." He didn't give all the reasons, from short supplies to the thought that Blackie could be looking for them.

"I know. Let's go."

Two hours later both Tad and Yvette were staggering, but they'd reached the edge of the trees and he stopped. "We'll spend the night here." It was early, but clearly, the two of them were spent and couldn't go further. Before them lay the rolling plains they had to cross to reach the fort. It would take a long time walking. What had happened to Blackie's horses? They sure could use something to ride.

Yvette and Tad sank to the ground, their exhaustion evident.

Gil stood beside Sam as he looked out at the hills before him. There would be no place to hide once they left the trees. But he might find a ranch closer than the fort. He squinted into the distance. Saw a movement. A horse and rider. Even knowing he would be invisible with the trees behind him, he drew back, pulling Gil with him.

"Is it Uncle?" Gil whispered.

"Can't tell." Sam returned to the others. "We won't have a fire tonight." Even though it meant they couldn't cook fish or warm themselves throughout the night.

"What is it?" Yvette asked.

He shook his head. He didn't want to worry her or Tad.

Yvette got to her feet and caught his hand, pulling him back to the viewpoint. "What is it?" she repeated.

He didn't answer.

She still held his hand and gave it a little shake. "I have the right to know. After all, we're in this together."

"Together?" The word rattled up his throat.

"Yes," She was very firm about it. "The rich girl is your partner whether or not you like it." The look in her eyes was his undoing. Demanding and longing intertwined.

"I think I like it." More than she would ever know. More than he had a right to.

"Very well." She looked out at the landscape before them. "What did you see?"

"Maybe it's what I don't see."

"You're stalling."

He stood behind her and pointed over her shoulder. "What do you see?"

"Grassy hills. Where's the fort?"

"Over the last hill."

She laughed. "That's very unconcise."

"Let's just say it's a long walk with little shelter."

She stiffened. "Is that a rider?"

"It is." He let the words sit in the silence, saying all that was needed.

"Is it Blackie?" She shuddered and her voice thinned.

"No way to tell." But the rider seemed to be coming in their direction.

"I see why you don't want a fire." She leaned back into his touch. "Are we ever going to be shed of that man?"

"We can't be sure it's him." He wanted to reassure her, but until they reached safety and reported Blackie's actions and he was in jail, they would all be watching over their shoulders, wondering if he would suddenly appear.

She turned so fast he caught her in his arms to hold her steady. "Sam, I'm so glad you are here with me... us." She put her hand to his cheek. Her touch made him aware of his unshaven state. And of the gentleness of her palm.

Reminded him of his dream.

He would not speak of it or think of it. Instead...

"I remember how safe I felt with my pa when we were caught in a snowstorm one time." He could not for the life of him explain why he'd mentioned that or why he'd suddenly remembered it. "Guess it has nothing to do with present circumstances."

"Maybe it does. Maybe you learned how much it meant to know your father would take care of you and now you are doing the same for us. Thank you, Sam. I believe your parents would be very proud of you."

Those words filled him with a longing that reached into his past and dragged forth all sorts of denied feelings. Of being valued. Of being important and loved. He crushed her to his chest and held her tight as the memories raged through him.

She must surely wonder at his behavior, but she said nothing. Her arms went around his waist and she held him tight.

After a moment, his feelings subsided and he relaxed his hold on her. She kept her arms around him, still as tight as ever.

She tipped her head back to look into his face. "Sam, you're a good man."

"Thanks." He wasn't sure what she meant. A good man because he'd taken care of her. A good man because he knew how to fish. A good man--

His tone must have given him away.

She hugged him tighter. "Sam, don't you think it's about time you started believing it?"

"I allowed my sister to believe I wrote her letters when I didn't."

"True. You maybe should have told her the truth sooner, but I know you did it with the best of intentions and I can't fault you for that."

"Really?"

She chuckled softly, the sound echoing in his chest, tickling his lungs so that he chuckled too.

"That's better," she said. She touched his lips. "You have a nice laugh."

He studied her face, let his gaze linger on her lips. He might like to kiss her. Except he had no right and he backed away. "Let's see what we can find to eat."

YVETTE DROPPED HER ARMS, feeling cold and alone. For a moment she thought Sam would kiss her. She would welcome it. Like she said, he was a good man. A man who was willing to take care of two boys and a city girl. A man who put others first. But also a man who did not see his own worth except as a cowboy. Not that she had anything against cowboys.

She joined him where they'd left the children. He was pulling things from the backpack that she'd discovered grew surprisingly heavy in a short time.

"Peaches and canned beans," he said as he held the two cans aloft. "I think we'll save the last of the jerky for tomorrow."

Yvette knew what he didn't add, that they were perilously close to being out of food. And miles of grassy hills to cross. And maybe Blackie to hide from. Was that rider still headed their way or had he turned another direction? If it was Blackie, she didn't think he would give up until he recaptured her and also retrieved the bundle of money in the backpack.

Sam opened the cans with his knife and divided the food among the four of them. When she noticed that he took a smaller portion, tears rolled from her eyes.

He looked at her, saw the dampness on her cheeks. "Yvette, what's wrong?"

She shook her head. "I'm just tired." There was no way she could explain how his unselfishness had affected her. All her life she'd felt like all that mattered about her was her family name and her father's money, but Sam sacrificed for her with no thought except to get her to safety.

Of course, her father would offer him a reward, but she doubted he'd even thought of that. Was he truly unconcerned about money? It hardly seemed possible, but Sam was so different than other men she'd met. In a very good way.

She waited until the boys were asleep and she and Sam had moved to the viewpoint. They sat side by side, looking out at the hills. She couldn't say if he looked for anything in particular, but she watched to see if a campfire glowed in the distance.

Nothing.

Sam stiffened. "Yvette, go back to the boys. Wake them and go hide in the trees. Don't make a sound."

At the tension in his voice, she rose silently, paused to see what had alarmed him. Seeing nothing, she slipped back to the boys.

And then she heard it. The gentle beat of horse's hooves. They'd been found. Somehow Blackie had gotten ahead of them and now returned for them.

She would run with the boys before she let him capture any of them again.

But what about Sam? She couldn't leave him at Blackie's mercy. Or rather, lack of it.

She hurried to Gil and Tad. Wakened them gently, her hand on each mouth to keep them from speaking.

"Come," she whispered. "We must hide."

Lord, keep Sam safe. And don't let the thunder of my frantic heart be heard by the rider.

13

Sam was on his feet, the long knife in his hand, waiting for the rider to reach him. He'd moved away from where Yvette and the boys waited in the hopes they could remain out of sight. A knife was little protection against any kind of a firearm, but it was all he had. But as long as he had breath, he meant to protect Yvette and the boys.

"Helloooo." The voice rang out. "Anyone there?"

Sure didn't sound like Blackie, but Sam wasn't about to fall for any tricks, so he remained silent.

The horse had stopped walking, so Sam reasoned it had reached the crest of the hill. The trees to his right blocked the rider from sight.

"Hello. I'm sure I saw someone. I mean you no harm. Just being neighborly." The horse snuffled. The tree branches rattled. The rider came into sight. He pulled to a halt and stared at Sam. "Howdy."

"How do," Sam said, every muscle tensed, ready to defend himself and the others.

"Allow me to introduce myself. Auss Wagner. I work for the Big Sky Ranch." He jabbed his thumb toward the east.

Sam remained poised for an attack as he studied the man before him. His piercing blue eyes were evident even in the fading light. He dressed more like a dude than a cowboy. He wore a fancy tweed jacket and a black bowler hat. But at his waist, Sam's opinion changed. Auss wore a hand-tooled gunbelt secured with leather tie-downs.

Sam swallowed hard. "Looks to me like you're a gunman." As soon as he said the words, he knew he should have kept his observation to himself.

Auss leaned over his saddle and chuckled. "A gun comes in handy from time to time." A beat of silence as if he expected Sam to have an opinion on the matter, but Sam kept his opinion to himself this time.

Auss shifted, his gaze barely leaving off Sam and yet Sam figured he'd seen everything. "What are you doing out here? Are you alone? Where's your horse?"

"You got a lot of questions for a stranger."

Auss's expression never changed, but his hand patted his holster. "Could shoot first. Ask questions later. But I don't work that way."

"Huh." There didn't seem much Sam could say in way of reply. Leastwise, nothing that he didn't think might offend the man.

"Let's try that again. Where's your horse?"

"Guess he's around somewhere."

"I saw the carcass of a bay horse by the river yesterday. Still had the saddle on. Guessing someone is missing it."

"Guess that would be so." They were doing a lot of guessing, but Sam wasn't ready to reveal anything to the man.

Auss sat up straight, the sudden move sending tension down Sam's spine.

"Time to get down to business." The hard note in Auss's voice could have cracked rocks.

Sam let the knife fall and held his hands out in a don't-shoot gesture. "I have no money." At least none that was his. "Nothing you'd want."

Auss sighed so long and hard, Sam wondered he didn't blow his teeth out. "Mister, if I wanted to rob someone, I wouldn't ride an hour up here. I'm only here because I thought you might need help. Guess I thought wrong." He lifted the reins and began to turn away.

Sam fought a fierce but short battle with himself. "Wait. I do need help."

Auss stopped. "Go on."

"Lost my horse and supplies a couple days back. Trying to get to the fort."

"Guess a horse might come in handy." Auss's statement sounded like a question. "Mine could carry two of us for a short distance. Maybe get us down to the ranch."

Sam didn't move.

Auss looked around. "You have anything you need to bring?"

Another short, intense argument was fought in Sam's brain. "I might have. Give me a minute."

"Sure thing." Auss relaxed in his saddle.

Sam hurried back to the others. "Someone's willing to help us."

Yvette watched him. Drew him aside. "What aren't you saying?"

"Am I that obvious?"

She shrugged. "Maybe I've learned to read you since we've spent so much time together."

The idea felt like a promise, but Sam didn't have time to dwell on it. Auss waited. "He looks like a gunfighter. I'm not sure I should trust him." He described the man to Yvette.

"I'm going to believe God has sent us a rescuer. Besides, now that he knows your whereabouts, he can follow you. Might as well be with him as looking over our shoulders to see if he's behind." She looked toward the east. "I didn't see much in the way of hiding places out there."

She made sense.

"If you're sure." He would have chosen some other means of help—a farming couple, or some of the boys from the Circle A. But what they had was a lone gunman.

She nodded.

"Stay close to me." He didn't have to tell the boys. They were practically glued to his heels. He held Yvette's hand as they returned to Auss.

Auss chuckled low in his throat when he saw them. "You didn't say you have an entire family with you."

Sam wasn't about to say otherwise and thankfully, no one else disabused Auss of his assumption. The four of them drew to a halt thirty feet from him.

Auss stroked his chin. "This kind of puts a knot in the idea of riding double back to the ranch." He studied them. "They look a mite wore out."

Sam slid his gaze toward the others. Yvette, her dress tattered and mud-stained and her hair tangled, did look like she'd fought a war with a wild cat. But her chin jutted out. Her hand tightened around his and he barely stopped himself from grinning. She might look battered, but her spirit was intact.

Tad had dark shadows under his eyes and looked like a strong wind would blow him out to the prairies. Gil, although as rumpled and stained as the rest of them, stood tall, his eyes flashing, prepared to defend his little brother if it was needed.

"It's been a difficult few days," Sam allowed. To say the least.

"Don't be alarmed. I'm going to get down." Auss didn't move for a heartbeat and then swung from his saddle, landing so he faced them. Sam guessed it was something a gunman learned—never turn your back on anyone.

"I've got supplies. You're welcome to them while I go back and get horses. Three should do it."

"Two will be just fine," Sam said, mildly. "The boys will ride with us."

"Very well." He removed a sack from his saddle-bags. "Some food. It'll keep you until I return in the morning."

"Thank you." Sam took the sack.

"I'll be on my way then. Stay safe." And with that, Auss mounted and rode down the hill.

The four of them watched until he was a good way off.

"I'm hungry," Gil said.

"Then let's eat." They sat on the crest of the hill. Sam opened the sack. The man must have a big appetite, as there were four thick roast-beef sandwiches, a sack of cookies, and some jam-filled biscuits. There'd be plenty for breakfast as well. They ate eagerly as they continued to watch Auss ride away.

"You think he'll come back?" Tad asked.

Sam guessed it was a question uppermost in the minds of all of them. "I think he will. But if he doesn't, we're better off than we were. We've at least got a bit of food."

When Auss was nothing but an indistinguishable dot in the distance, they returned to where they'd left their things. The boys rolled up in their blankets and waited to hear stories from Yvette and Sam.

Yvette told the Bible story of the one lost sheep. "I think Jesus has found us just like the shepherd did." Her voice choked. "God is good."

Sam told about the time one of the newborn colts had been missing. "Maude and John warned me some wild animal had likely taken it. But I refused to give up. It took me two days, but I found him. He'd fallen into a little hollow and couldn't get out."

The boys fell asleep.

Sam and Yvette returned to the viewpoint. Darkness filled the valleys. Moonlight highlighted the hills and shimmered off the waving grass. A tiny flash of orange in the distance made him think it might be the ranch to which Auss headed and he pointed it out to Yvette.

"This time tomorrow we should be at the fort," he said. Regret tinted his words. Not that he didn't want to get them all to safety, but once they were back with others, he would be a cowboy, she would be the rich city girl.

"I hope Blackie isn't there." She shivered.

Not knowing if she was cold or afraid, not that knowing would have made him do anything different, he put an arm around her and pulled her close.

"I don't think he'd tried anything with the place full of Mounties."

"I suppose that's true."

"And we'll report him for kidnapping. That's a hanging offense."

She shivered again.

His arm tightened around her. "Sorry. I shouldn't have upset you by telling you that."

"You didn't." She lifted her face to him. "You won't leave us when we get there, will you?"

He touched her cheek. In his mind, she was part of his dream. A home, children, and a woman who filled his house and heart with love. It would be so easy to kiss her. To let his feelings tell him what to do. But he couldn't take advantage of the situation.

He never wanted to leave her, but how realistic was that. But like he'd said, it was an impossible dream. "I'll see that you get where you need to be." Even if it meant letting her go to a man looking for a mail-order bride. Of course, her bit of newspaper was gone. Would she give up on that foolish idea or find another newspaper with another ad in it?

He felt her air release. She shifted ever so slightly, but he felt it as clearly as if she'd hurried back to the boys.

His heart squeezed out a painful beat. Already she was leaving him. And it hurt.

How would he survive a final goodbye?

Yvette couldn't bring herself to leave the shelter of his arms even though he had not offered her what she practically begged for. *Don't leave us. Don't leave me.*

How much plainer could she be?

She'd grown close to him these last few days. Was he only being nice, protective, and kind because that was who he was? She had no doubt he would have been so with anyone and yet so often she'd felt a special connection to him. She didn't want to return to being Yvette Bellamy, the rich man's daughter. Nor did she want to write to someone who had an advertisement in the paper. She knew what she wanted. To be the woman that she'd been these last few days. Brave, independent, accepted as an equal, protected without being coddled, and a partner in facing challenges.

Obviously, he didn't feel the same.

She made no attempt to hide a yawn. It provided a perfect excuse for pleading tiredness and curling up in her blanket. The day had taken a physical toll on her and she slept despite the regret scraping at her brain.

The next morning she awakened with the knowledge they would soon be at the fort and things would change so much. Not wanting to think about it, she said little as they prepared to leave.

Sam must have noticed her quietness. He asked if there was anything the matter.

"No."

Tad looked at her with big eyes, full of tenderness. Oh, what a lovely child he was. Somehow, she must convince everyone that she was the appropriate person to raise them.

He smiled so sweetly it made her eyes sting, then he turned to Sam. "She's afraid we can't be family when we get to the fort."

Yvette coughed, tears threatening to overflow her eyes. She ducked her head so Sam couldn't see her face and pulled Tad to her lap. "I'm going to get you and Gil. We will be family."

"Sam, too?" Tad asked.

Yvette didn't answer, waiting…hoping…Sam would say something. He didn't.

Gil pulled Tad from Yvette's arms. "We aren't going back to Uncle."

"Of course you aren't." Yvette and Sam said as one.

At least they were agreed on that matter.

Gil stood before them, holding Tad's hand. "I'll work for someone so long as they'll let Tad be with me."

Yvette reached for them, wanting to hold them close to her heart, but Gil backed away.

He turned to Tad. "We don't need family. We'll make it on our own."

Yvette's heart broke into a hundred unsalvageable pieces. Gil wasn't very big and here he was fighting to be independent. She would do the same.

Only one thing would persuade her to give up the freedom she'd found—at the Circle A as well as being with Sam these past days—and Sam didn't seem to be about to offer that.

Part of her wanted to argue with Gil—persuade him that he could have a family. But she couldn't even offer that. Unless…

But Sam had been given plenty of opportunity to say something if he wanted to create a family. There was no point in beating a dead horse.

By the time they'd eaten the food Auss had left and packed up everything in preparation for leaving—a task that took all of five minutes—they heard Auss in the distance calling, "Good morning."

They went to the crest of the hill to watch him ride toward them.

Gil, still holding Tad's hand, stood a few feet away, making it obvious he meant for the two of them to manage on their own.

Yvette stood close enough to Sam that he could have reached for her hand if he wanted.

He didn't make a move toward her.

It seemed all of them were prepared to go their separate ways.

They would each take a fragment of her heart when they did.

SHE RODE astride the horse Auss provided with Gil at her back. Tad rode behind Sam. None of them had said a word since they began the ride to the fort.

They stopped for a brief break when the sun was at its zenith. Auss handed around sandwiches.

"Talkative bunch, aren't you?"

Sam was the only one inclined to answer. "Guess we're weary."

"Yup. Guess so." Auss shook his head.

The fort came into sight shortly after they resumed riding, but it was two more hours before they rode down the dusty street of the little town. They stopped in front of the mercantile.

"Figure you folks might be wanting some new duds and a bath in that order. You can buy ready-mades here and over there"—he jabbed his thumb down the street—"is a boarding house where the missus can get a bath. You fellows might be better off over there." He pointed toward a sign that said bathhouse. "Do you have funds to pay for all that? If not, I can lend you some."

"We're fine," Sam said. "Thanks for your help."

The four of them stood in front of the store as Auss led the horses away.

"Pick out what you need. This is on Blackie." Sam chuckled.

Realizing the humor of Blackie's money buying them all new clothes, Yvette grinned.

They went inside, the boys and Sam going to the men's section while Yvette went to the back where the ladies' wear was displayed. Several dresses were in her size. One made out of fine satin with ruffles on the bodice, a flounce at the back. The one beside it was a simple cotton dress such as worn by the farm women she'd seen. She had no trouble choosing the latter. It was in keeping with the changes she meant to implement in her life.

Sam paid for it all. "Do you want to meet again after we're cleaned up?"

Did he really have to ask? "Do you think Blackie's stash would provide us with a decent meal?"

His eyes twinkled. He looked up and down the street. Saw a dining room sign. "Shall we meet over there in an hour?"

"Excellent. I can't wait." And she didn't mean just for the food. She hadn't given up the idea of a shared future. A family. As she hurried toward the boarding house Auss had indicated, she realized that what she wanted was marriage. Did she love him enough to marry him?

The answer was easy. She did.

The bigger question was, did he love her? Or was he willing to marry with the hopes love would grow? Wasn't that what a mail-order marriage entailed?

A little later she lay back in a tub of warm, scented water. Never had such a simple thing felt like such a luxury. She might have stayed longer, except the water grew cold and she didn't want to call for more hot water. And she was due to meet Sam soon.

A tremor raced across her skin as she dressed. She knew what she wanted to say to him. But she couldn't find the words to express what was in her heart. *God, give me the words.*

She retired to the back step and sat in the sun, brushing her hair to dry it.

A noise came from the other side of the house. She recognized Gil's voice. Had they come for her? Her hair was still damp, but she could pin it up and let it dry.

The door beside her opened and two boys faced her. Their eyes were wide, wild. She jumped to her feet.

"What's wrong?"

"Sam's in jail."

14

"I did not kidnap her." Sam had said the words so many times and still, no one would believe him. "Would I come riding into town with her if I had?"

The suit-clad man who'd escorted the Mountie to where Sam had just finished dressing after his bath, shrugged. "Who knows what a man like you would do? All I know is Mr. Bellamy got a note demanding money for Miss Yvette's release. Instructions were to meet the low-down scum here. I've been cooling my heels for days."

It seemed the man didn't care for having to spend time at the fort. Sam snorted under his breath. He should have tried being stranded in the woods with nothing but the clothes on his back.

"I'm innocent."

"You can defend yourself at the trial." The man had reluctantly given his name at Sam's query as Mr. Flinn.

Sam thought he should have been named Flint because he was hard and not about to admit he might be wrong. The Mountie had no choice but to take Mr. Flinn's accusations seriously and put him in jail where he sat on the edge of a hard cot provided for prisoners in the narrow, musty-smelling cell. His worries seemed overwhelming. What if Blackie was hiding out in the town and followed Yvette? Where were the boys? He had not felt so helpless since the day he'd been escorted to the orphanage. All he could do was pray. And trust God. He bowed his head into his palms and prayed that Yvette and the boys would be protected.

A short time later, he heard a clatter in the adjacent room where a Mountie was keeping watch.

"He's innocent. Let him out."

At the sound of Yvette's voice, Sam was on his feet. She'd set everything straight. A draft across the floor and a thud suggested the door had again opened and closed. Sam recognized the rumble of a male voice as that of Mr. Flinn's. He couldn't hear everything that was said but caught enough to know that Mr. Flinn argued with Yvette.

Smiling, Sam waited at the bars. Yvette was used to issuing orders and having them obeyed. He had no doubt that she would prevail. Sure enough, the adjoining door opened and the Mountie strode in. He unlocked the door.

"You're a free man."

Ignoring the scowl on Mr. Flinn's face, Sam hurried to Yvette's side. "Thank you. Where are the boys?"

"They're waiting outside." She squeezed his arm. She took in his new jeans and buff-colored shirt. "You look different than you did. I like it."

He liked what he saw too. She wore a dark blue dress that made her eyes appear browner. Her shiny brown hair was pinned in a roll at the back of her neck.

The Mountie returned to his desk, saving Sam from making a fool of himself by staring at Yvette like no one else existed. "Now tell me what happened."

Sam and Yvette took turns relaying their adventure as the Mountie made notes.

The Mountie looked up. "You haven't seen this Blackie since you fell in the river?"

"No." Sam glanced toward the outer door. "I won't feel like Yvette is safe so long as he's at large."

The Mountie bent over the paper again. "Can you give me a description of the man and what he was wearing?"

Yvette didn't give Sam a chance to speak. "He was dirty. Long, scraggly black hair. His trousers were so dirty they could have stood by themselves. Their original color of gray was mostly hidden beneath the layers of dirt. And the shirt he wore—" She shuddered. "It might have originally been white but it's hard to tell. There was a tear in the left elbow that he'd repaired with what looked like horse hair."

Sam stared at her. How had she noticed all those things?

The Mountie rose and went to the nearby cupboard. He pulled out a bundle, unfolded it on the desk top. "Would these be his clothes?" He held up the shirt, turning it so the left sleeve was visible.

Yvette stepped behind Sam as if needing him to protect her from Blackie. "Those are his. Where is he?"

"These items were found on a man washed up on the banks of the river. From what you've said, I would conclude that it was Blackie." He put the bundle of clothes back in the cupboard and returned to the desk.

"He's dead?" Yvette sounded more shocked than relieved.

"You won't need to worry about him again," the Mountie said.

Yvette seemed speechless at this news.

"What about the boys?" Sam asked. "What's to become of them?"

Leaning back in his chair, the Mountie studied Sam and then Yvette. "From what you say, it seems there is no other family. I can think of no better place for them than to go with you. You can give them a good home."

You? Did he mean Sam or Yvette? And then the truth hit Sam. The Mountie assumed Sam and Yvette were man and wife.

"We aren't married."

The Mountie lowered his chair to all fours. "That doesn't change things a whole lot. Either they go with one of you or I take them to the orphanage."

Sam was not about to allow Gil and Tad to go to any orphanage, but before he could give words to his thoughts, Yvette spoke out.

"I've already said I'll take them. I can afford to give them a good home."

Sam held back his words, but it seemed money mattered when it came to such choices.

The Mountie waved them away. "I'll leave it to you."

"What about the money in Blackie's pack?" Sam asked.

"It belongs to the boys now. It can be used to raise them."

Flinn had been leaning against the wall watching the proceedings. He hurried to Yvette's side. "I have orders to see that you get back home. My orders don't include children."

Yvette drew herself up, as regal as a queen. "The boys belong in the west. I believe I do too. I won't be going back." She stared the man down.

"We'll see about this." Angry strides took him out the door.

Yvette tucked her hand into the crook of Sam's elbow. "Let's go eat."

He couldn't fight her for the boys. What did he

have to offer them in comparison to her? But at least she said she was staying in the west. He could hope to visit them. But he knew it wouldn't be enough to satisfy the place in his heart created especially for the three of them.

The boys waited outside and patted Sam.

"Glad they let you go," Gil said.

"We knew Yvette would make them," Tad said with such confidence that Sam and Yvette chuckled.

"Your uncle will never shut you up in that cabin again," Yvette said. She indicated the nearby bench. She and Sam sat and together explained about Blackie.

"What happens to us now?" Gil asked.

"I'll keep you. We'll be a family."

Tad hugged her, but Gil stood back, his gaze going from Sam to Yvette. "What about Sam? Isn't he part of our family?"

Sam's insides bled so fiercely he wouldn't have been shocked to see blood pool at his feet. What could he say to the boy?

He let Yvette answer.

"I'm sure we'll see lots of him. If that's what he wants."

He stared at Yvette. "What I want is to see the boys every day." *And you.* But he couldn't add the last two words. He remembered the many times he'd been told he was wasting people's time. The only place he hadn't felt it was true was at the ranch. Would Yvette choose to live there? She hadn't said and he didn't want to shatter any possibility it could happen by asking.

It was a quiet quartet that sat in the dining room. The roast beef, mashed potatoes and gravy, carrots, and beet pickles were delicious and they all ate heartily. But no one seemed inclined to talk.

Sam wanted to know about Yvette's plans for herself and the boys but didn't have the courage to ask. Instead, he asked, "Are you going to find another newspaper and look for another man to write to? You know, as a mail-order bride?"

She gave him a look he couldn't identify. He only knew it made his mouth go dry as sand. Then her eyebrows lifted so slightly he wondered if he'd imagine it.

"I'm not going to write to anyone. I've decided—"

Before she could finish Mr. Flinn strode up to their table. "Miss Bellamy, I have wired your father. He insists you come home immediately. You'll leave on the morning train with an appropriate chaperone."

Sam's heart reverberated off his ribs. He wanted to rush her out of the dining room and away from this man. But Yvette alone would have to make her wishes clear.

Yvette rose to her feet, as regal in bearing as if she ruled the world. "Mr. Flinn, I have told you my decision and I haven't changed my mind."

Mr. Flinn took a step back and then one forward.

Seeing the look of fury on the man's face, Sam rose and stood close enough to Yvette to signal he would protect her.

"Miss, you can't." The man sputtered the words out. "I have orders from your father."

"I will write a letter to my father explaining everything. Now go away and let us finish in peace." She dismissed him with a wave of her hand.

Mr. Flinn made another appeal. "Your father also said he would not support you financially if you insisted on this foolishness."

"I understand."

Sam wondered if she truly did. Money would be important if she meant to make a home for the boys. Of course, she could marry—the word jammed a log in further thought.

Flinn looked about ready to eat his hat, then rushed from the room.

Sam and Yvette returned to their seats. The boys watched with startled expressions.

Yvette chuckled. "Did you think I would leave you two?"

Tad shook his head. Gil looked pleased.

Yvette's gaze came to Sam. "I'm not leaving." Her gaze riveted him.

He couldn't move. Couldn't think. What did it mean that she wasn't planning to leave? Did she plan to live at the fort? Raise the boys there? Under cover of the table, his fists curled and uncurled. He didn't want any of them at the fort.

He wanted them at the Circle A where he could see them every day.

Could she be persuaded to go there? But what would she do?

She could be a wife, a little voice whispered. *Your wife.*

He swallowed hard. Twice. Would she even consider such a thing? What did he have to offer her? Besides his heart. But that was not enough. She needed a home. A fine home with fine things. He thought of the cabin Maude was having built at the ranch. It would be the third new cabin in a matter of months. Maude had this notion that all her 'boys' needed to be married. He and Pete were the last of the boys and he figured Maude expected Pete to move into the new cabin with a wife of his own. After all, Pete was older.

But Pete's age wasn't the biggest hindrance.

Sam wanted a wife who loved him. Flaws notwithstanding. But even greater concern was knowing Yvette deserved far better than him.

But if she was willing to seek a mail-order marriage, maybe…just maybe…she'd be willing to give him a chance.

A chance to do what? Prove he couldn't write worth a bean? Didn't have anything to offer besides a small cabin? Or would she see it as a way to give the boys a family?

He'd ask before he lost his nerve. He gathered up his courage. "Boys, would you wait over by the window while Yvette and I talk?"

Gil gave him a hard look as if to demand that he make this work for all of them.

Tad's eyes also begged Yvette to make things right.

Then the pair moved away.

Sam leaned forward. "Yvette, if you marry me, you and I can make a home for the boys. I think that would be in their best interests, don't you? What do you say? Will you marry me?"

For a woman who had just been offered marriage, she didn't look pleased. Well, what did he expect? He waited, his gaze riveted to her, his heart refusing to beat. His head began to swim.

"I'll take care of them. There's the money and… I'll go visit Grace while I sort things out."

"We could do it together." He wasn't above pleading his cause.

Yvette shook her head. "There was a time I thought I could marry someone just to escape my life back home but, thanks to you, I realize I have the ability to stand on my own two feet. Sam, I don't need to marry to take care of the boys."

He sought in vain for arguments, but his brain could only focus on one thing. She'd said no. She didn't need him.

The dining room door opened and two cowboys clattered in and headed for his table.

The boys hurried back to stand at his side, eyes wide and watchful.

"You sure are a hard man to find," Pete said.

"Glad to see you're safe," Adam added. His gaze rested on the boys. "How do you do that? Leave home with Miss Yvette, disappear and then show up with two good-sized boys."

Adam and Pete pulled up chairs and ordered food. As they ate, Sam and Yvette provided details.

"Maude and John will be anxious to know you're both safe. We need to get back as soon as possible. Guess you don't have a horse, Sam. We'll buy one and leave in the morning."

"Do you mind getting a wagon or buggy?" Yvette said. "I'm planning to go too. And the boys. I'm going to keep them."

Pete and Adam looked at each other. It was Adam who spoke. "I know you'll be most welcome."

Sam had still not had a coherent thought. All he knew was he'd be able to see Yvette and the boys. The thought was as bitter as it was sweet.

"We'll find something," Pete said. "Are we all agreed to leave first thing in the morning?" He and Adam got to their feet and headed for the door.

"Excuse me," Sam said to Yvette and followed them outside.

As soon as the door closed behind him, the two

stopped him in his tracks.

Pete gave Sam a look that threatened to fry his insides "You need to do the right thing and marry her. You've been alone with her for days. Doesn't she deserve to have her name protected?"

"You consider that reason enough to marry?" Adam said, giving Pete a look of disbelief.

"I already asked her. She said no." The words caught in his throat.

Adam sighed. "What did you say? What reason did you give for asking to marry her?"

"I said we could give the boys a home."

"Sam, there is only one good reason to get married. Because you love her and can't imagine life without her."

"I love her so much it scares me. I can't imagine life without her. But what do I have to offer? I don't even have a home of my own." What gripped him was not his lack of possessions so much as it was his personal lacks. He was a good cowboy, but his deficiencies as a human had been drilled into him, first by a teacher and later by the staff at the orphanage. Having several adoptive families reject him only reinforced his feelings of inadequacy. His heart would refuse to function if he heard any of those words from Yvette. Yet, if he continued to hide from the hurt, he would never be whole, ready to be a husband and father.

It was a huge risk to consider taking

Pete chuckled. "There's a cabin almost finished on

the ranch. And have you forgotten you are co-owner of the Circle A? But all that aside—" He broke off and stared past Sam. He nudged Adam and they sauntered away.

Sam didn't have to turn to know Yvette stood behind him.

How much had she heard? He continued to face forward as he gathered together his thoughts. Did he have something to offer her? Was his love enough? Slowly he turned, hat in hand.

Some risks were worth taking.

Yvette didn't see anyone but Sam. She hadn't meant to eavesdrop, but when she realized they talked about her, she couldn't help herself. "You love me?"

A passing couple gave her a startled look.

She took Sam's arm. "Let's find a place where we can talk in private."

They went down a side street to a quiet, deserted piece of land and stopped under a tree.

She faced him, her heart beating extra fast then stalling as she waited to hear the words he'd spoken to Adam. "Tell me what you said to the others."

He studied her face, his gaze searched hers. She opened her heart and let it speak through her eyes. Knew the moment it did.

"I'm nothing but—"

She placed two fingers on his lips. "I don't want to ever hear that again. You are a good, kind man with many skills. Without your knowledge, we would have perished."

He nodded but still didn't say the words she longed for.

She cradled his face in her palms. "Sam, tell me what's in your heart."

He took her hands and pulled them to his chest, holding them against the spot where she could feel the steady thump of his heart. "Yvette, I love you. I want to spend the rest of my life with you."

She laughed with sheer joy. "I love you too. Forever and always."

A wide smile replaced the uncertainty in his face.

"I have no home. No—"

"Sam, I would live in the woods with you. Oh, wait. I did. Maybe something better than that, but I'm truly not fussy. I found what I want sharing life with you. Sam, you are everything I need and want in a man." Joy rose within her as she watched her words reach into his heart and heal the wounds caused by the unkindness of others. "I believe the hurts inflicted on you have made you into a finer, stronger, kinder, better man than most."

"Then I am glad I received them. Yvette, will you marry me?"

"Yes, yes. A thousand times yes." She lifted her face to him.

His kiss was everything she could wish for, everything she'd ever dreamed. Sweet as candy, soft as morning dew, and lingering with promises for the future.

He lifted his head. "Where are the boys?"

"I ordered dessert for them and told them to wait for me."

"Good." He kissed her again. "Let's find them and give them the news. Then find Adam and Pete." They began to walk back when he pulled her to a halt. "When do you want to get married?"

She knew from Grace and Adam's wedding that a preacher would have to be called to the ranch if they were married there. However, there was a preacher here. Even if he was away, there were Mounties authorized to officiate at a marriage. "Can we marry here before we go to the ranch?"

"Here? Now? Are you sure?"

"I can't think of a single reason to wait."

He whooped. "Neither can I."

They found the boys and told them. Tad hugged her. Gil patted Sam's back and said he approved. Sam pulled Gil into his arms. She caught a glint of tears in the eyes of both the man and the boy. Felt a sting in her own eyes.

They rejoined Pete and Adam and informed them of their decision. Both seemed to approve. They conferred for a few minutes then each went to do their part in making the wedding happen.

. . .

THEY MET at the church at the appointed time.

"I wired my parents," Yvette said. "I told them I was being married." She'd also said, "Please be happy for me. Letter to follow." Then she'd written a long missive telling them about Sam and Gil and Tad.

She'd purchased three more dresses. One was silvery gray, perfect for an unplanned wedding.

Sam had taken care of getting enough clothing for the boys. They waited in front of the church, grinning from ear to ear.

Adam and Pete were inside and smiled as Yvette and Sam entered arm in arm.

Sam and Yvette exchanged vows and were declared husband and wife. As they kissed, Pete hooted, Adam clapped and the boys hugged them.

To her surprise, Sam had rented a nice room at the hotel and informed her the boys were staying with Adam and Pete. As they lay arm in arm, she sighed. "I never thought to be this happy."

"This is my dream come true," he murmured.

"You never did tell me your dream."

"To have a home of my own complete with a wife who loves me despite my shortcomings and to have children."

"I am totally unaware of any shortcomings." Her tone was very firm. "You are everything I need and want."

EPILOGUE

Tad ran into the house. Yvette smiled at the boy and looked around. Her house. Hers and Sam's and the boys. The cabin was finished a few days after they returned to the ranch and since then had been expanded by two more bedrooms.

"For future plans," Sam had said, kissing her soundly as the little boys watched.

"Someone's coming," Tad said.

"Company for Uncle John and Aunt Maude, I suppose." Yvette pulled four golden loaves of bread from the oven and tipped them out on a rack to cool. She smiled. Content with her life, pleased with her growing ability to cook and bake, and happily in love with Sam. A love that deepened with every passing day.

"Uncle John is waving this way."

Yvette lifted the lid on the pot of stew that

simmered on the back of the stove and gave the contents a stir.

"Is it Ilsa coming to visit Aunt Beth?"

"No. It's a man and woman and they're stopping here." Tad rushed from the window and over to the table, sitting on a chair furthest from the door.

"Here? Who could it be?" Yvette knew no one apart from those at the ranch and Ilsa and Abner in Logan Crossing. She wiped her hands on the nearby towel, untied her apron and hung it on a hook by the cupboard, then went to see who it was.

"It's my parents. Tad, run and get Sam and your brother." She rushed outside to greet them. There was a moment of awkwardness. Her first instinct was to throw herself in their arms, but they weren't that kind of people.

But she was. She'd grown into the person she now was and hugged her mother. "I'm so glad to see you." Then she hugged her father. "Both of you."

She stepped back, smiling her welcome. "Come in and see my home." Did they notice that she called it home, not house? They followed her inside.

"Fresh bread," her mother said. "It smells so good. Who made it?"

"I did." Her satisfaction at conquering the task fled a bit. Then resurfaced. She knew how challenging it had been and was pleased with the results.

Mother blinked. "You can bake bread?"

"I can bake bread and cakes and cookies. I can

make a good meal. Can you smell the stew in that pot? I made it."

Apart from his initial greeting, Father had not said anything. Now he did. "This is where you live?"

"Yes, isn't it charming?"

"It's small," he said.

"I prefer to think of it as cozy. Come and see the rest." She pointed out the table. "This is where we eat our meals. Sam built the table and benches. Aren't they lovely?" She hurried them into the next room. "Our sitting room." There were two rocking chairs Maude had ordered for them, a little settee in dark green, and a bookcase with several books. Despite the fact that Sam had trouble writing, he had no trouble reading and enjoyed it. They spent many pleasant hours reading to the boys and each other. But she didn't share that detail with her parents. Instead, she pointed to the green drapes with tiny red roses trailing down the fabric. "I made all the curtains in the house." She didn't care if she sounded pleased with herself.

She led them down the hall to the bedrooms. "This is where Sam and I sleep." A beautiful quilt covered the bed. "The ladies here made it for us."

"It's very nice," her mother said.

It was the first thing either of them had said about her home. At least it was positive.

"Tad and Gil sleep here." She opened the door to the second room, thankful she'd made both beds this morning. "And this is our spare room. You're welcome to stay here with us."

They returned to the kitchen. Yvette made tea and served slices of warm bread and butter sprinkled with sugar and cinnamon.

"I'm glad you've come," she said.

"We've come to take you home," her father said.

Before Yvette could protest, her mother spoke. "We've come to make sure you're happy and I see you are."

The door opened and Sam entered with the boys.

"Mother, Father, this is my husband, Sam, and my boys, Tad and Gil."

Sam looked worried, but Yvette smiled and nodded and he relaxed.

Her parents stayed with them for a week. At first, they were awkward with the others, but John and Maude soon put them at ease and the other families entertained them.

Yvette confided to Sam that she had never seen her parents so relaxed.

The day before they were due to leave, her parents asked to talk to Sam and Yvette. The four of them sat around the table.

Yvette tried not to be apprehensive as she suspected her father had something serious to say to them.

Her father began. "Yvette, we are relieved to see

you so happy, but after time, struggling to survive can become tiresome."

"Father—" She had to tell him that life was so much more meaningful and enjoyable when there was a purpose to what she did.

He held up a hand. "Let me finish. Sam, you are a hardworking man. I admire that. The boys seem like fine fellows. We've decided we'd like to help by giving you five thousand dollars with more to come each year."

Sam jerked to his feet. "I can take care of my family."

Yvette caught his hand and pulled him down. "Father, thank you, but we don't need your money. I love life with challenges. And a man who cares about me."

"I meant no insult," Father said. "Is there nothing we can do to help?"

"I have an idea," Yvette said. "Let me talk to Sam about it." They stepped from the house and Yvette explained what she was thinking.

Sam grinned. "I like it."

They returned. "Mother, Father, if you want to do something to help, you could build a schoolhouse so all these children here could have some proper learning."

Father grinned. "I like that idea. I'll speak to John and Maude to get their agreement. What's more, I'll pay the teacher's salary until these boys of yours are through school."

"And beyond if there are more children," Mother added.

Maude and John were more than agreeable. "We'll call it the Bellamy school." John and Father sat together drawing out plans and discussing where the school would go.

As her parents departed the next morning, Yvette said to Sam, "I've never seen them so happy."

He draped an arm across her shoulders to pull her close. "And I'm guessing they could say the same about you."

"That could be because I have never ever been so happy. And it's all thanks to you and two little boys."

As if knowing they were being talked about, Gil and Tad came to them. Sam drew them into a group hug.

"Dreams do come true," he murmured.

ALSO BY LINDA FORD

Historical Romance

Love on the Western Trail

Renewed Love

Rescued Love

Reluctant Love

Redeemed Love

Romancing the West

Jake's Honor

Cash's Promise

Blaze's Hope

Levi's Blessing

A Heart's Yearning

A Heart's Blessing

A Heart's Delight

A Heart's Promise

Sunny Ridge, Montana

Rodeo and Juliet

Glory, Montana

Loving a Rebel

A Love to Cherish

Renewing Love

A Love to Have and Hold

Cowboy Father

Cowboy Groom

Cowboy Preacher

Rancher's Bride

Hunter's Bride

Christmas Bride

Love on the Santa Fe Trail

Wagon Train Baby

Wagon Train Wedding

Wagon Train Matchmaker

Wagon Train Christmas

Dakota Brides series

Temporary Bride

Abandoned Bride

Second-Chance Bride

Reluctant Bride

War Brides series

Lizzie

Maryelle

Irene

Grace

<u>Wild Rose Country</u>

Crane's Bride

Hannah's Dream

Chastity's Angel

Cowboy Bodyguard

Contemporary Romance

<u>Montana Skies series</u>

Cry of My Heart

Forever in My Heart

Everlasting Love

Inheritance of Love

Copyright © 2020 by Linda Ford

All rights reserved.

No part of this book may be reproduced in any form or by any electronic or mechanical means, including information storage and retrieval systems, without written permission from the author, except for the use of brief quotations in a book review.

Made in United States
Cleveland, OH
17 February 2025